JOSEPH McGEE PRIVATE INVESTIGATOR:
BOOK NINE

INTERNATIONAL CAUSE CÉLÈBRE OF IVORY WHITE

Conspiracy, Crime, and a Major Fight, Waged in Secret

By
CARL DOUGLASS

Neurosurgeon Turned Author Writes With
Gripping Realism

PUBLICATION
CONSULTANTS
We Believe In The Power Of Authors

PO Box 221974 Anchorage, Alaska 99522-1974
books@publicationconsultants.com—www.publicationconsultants.com

ISBN Number: 978-1-63747-120-3
eBook ISBN Number: 978-1-63747-078-7

Library of Congress Number: 2022948041

Manufactured in the United States of America

DISCLAIMER

All the novellas in the McGee Series are works of fiction and should not be construed as representing real persons, places, or events. Some names of real persons and places appear but only for the purpose of creating a setting in the real world or as a mention of historical circumstances. None of the real people or the real places were actually involved in the fictional portrayals found in these short books.

DEDICATION

To the lonely souls who work without thanks and often in peril, to bring an end to police, military, and governmental, corruption around the world.

CHAPTER
ONE

vory woke up face down on a filthy concrete floor accepting his condition as clear evidence that today was going to be a bad day. If he needed confirmation of that prophecy, he was a mass of bruises and pain from his clavicles to the tips of his toes. Oddly, his face had been spared. His head was swimming; he could smell blood–his blood–and he heard coarse Spanish epithets as the only communications going on in the dismal room.

It was not a room in the usual sense of the word. He was alone in a five by six feet windowless compartment with the only view outside obstructed by steel bars painted white with the paint peeling off and rust showing through on the door. It was a cell which was not as large as his half-bath at home.

The events of the previous day began slowly to come into focus as he became increasingly aware of those confusing circumstances and as he tried to force his foggy brain to do its job. He gradually began to remember being arrested and bundled off to the courthouse without hearing anything like a Miranda recitation of his rights. Apparently–from the experience thus far–he had none. He demanded to know the charges against him; and the cops and prosecutors just laughed.

Then the beatings started. Masked men slapped him, clubbed him with a heavy rubber hose, kicked his arms and legs, but avoided his face for some reason. Brutes with heavy military boots kicked at his groin; so, he curled up into a fetal ball and tried his best to move out of the way of blows aimed at his family jewels. He was only partly successful, and he painfully peed blood every time he urinated. Depending on either the short term or the long-term viewpoint, he was so dehydrated that urinations were not very frequent; so, the pain was also infrequent; but he worried about hematuria coming from injured kidneys which did not have enough fluid to keep good flow going; and he knew that his kidneys would not last long without hydration.

For the moment, his worry came in the form of four large ugly men in guard uniforms who burst into his tiny cell.

"¡Párate! Vienes con nosotros. ¡Ahora!" the senior guard shouted directly into Ivory's faces, spittle flying.

It was not a request. Ivory stood up, went with the guards, and did it at the double despite shafts of pain from every muscle as he tried to obey the part about, "Now!"

He was taken to a large room where nineteen other men stood with their backs to a blank light blue screen.

"Desnuda y ponte esta ropa," a guard shouted and handed him a clean and newly pressed prison shirt and pants.

Modesty was no longer a privacy he could hope for. He stripped and put on the clothes, including a shiny pair of slip-on faux patent leather black shoes. He was handed a sign to hold ing front of him which read, *"Acusado de pedófiloy el tráfico sexual infantil."* [Charged with pedophilia and child sex trafficking] in large bold lettering. The nineteen other inmates were evidently well-known prisoners to the news media, even in the United States. Their signs included official looking plaques bearing charges the same as Ivory's and others such as "Child rapist", "Child molester", "Trafficker of women and children", and "Corrupt Police Officer".

The sign over men near the ceiling of the prison wall read, "Federal Social Readaptation Center No. 1" and below that, "Altiplano maximum security prison, Almoloya de Juarez".

The charges were all related to the accusations against Ivory; there were no "thieves", "bank robbers", "burglars", or "perpetrators of domestic violence". Ivory presumed the photograph and the kinds of alleged crimes listed on the prison posters the men were holding were for the benefit of the American audience more than anyone else.

Within a day—with the help of *New York Times* and *Washington Post* front page stories with the photograph—McGee, Caitlin, the DCIA, and the president—were fully informed and appropriately incensed, as the Mexican president and senior law enforcement officers had intended.

President Willets read the news reports quickly and put in an immediate secure call to the president of Mexico.

"Mr. President, this is the President of the United States speaking. I was alarmed to read in the New York and Washington newspapers and to see on our television news stations that a well-respected US citizen has been thrown into jail on trumped up charges, and worse, that he is being held without the benefit of a defense attorney or without even hearing the charges against him. Please get him released at once, Sir."

"With due respect, Mr. President, allow me to correct some wrongful information you seem to have received. The man in question is called Ivory White, a gang leader from Harlem, New York. He was caught in the very act of trafficking by a task force of my handpicked officers. The idea floated by his followers is that the Mexican police are full of corruption, and he is a victim of such corrupt officers is patent nonsense. You would do well to root out the corruption in your own forces and halt the irresistible drug urge and desire to destroy young girls and boys among your own citizens before making brash accusations in your news media."

"Mr. President, we have enough evidence to convict you and your entire senior officer corps of the military, law enforcement, and government. In fact, if I do not see positive results within minutes of hanging up, I will announce to the world warrants from the US, the UK, Germany France, Scandinavia, and INTERPOL and its 194 member countries, effective this evening."

"You, sir, are bluffing. If you had evidence, you would have presented it before now. You and your country are just bullies, and I am standing up to you. Good day, Sir," and he hung up on the US president.

"Pathetic, corrupt, pip squeak. 'Bluffing', he says. The DOJ has a mountain of evidence about the corruption I described. I will begin to publish documents every day at noon and will have them broadcast through the US, Europe, and Asia, at the stroke of noon every day until I can shake Ivory White's hand in front of the world press against a background of huge posters spelling out his own involvement in the interdiction of trafficking for all to see," the president said to the assembled cabinet members.

Secretary of State, Corsill Abramson raised his right hand in a palm extended stop sign.

"Mr. President, a note of caution, if I may."

"Go ahead."

"We may suffer irreversible harm from President Sanchez-Porteño's blowback against us. I think the whole thing will blow over in a couple of days or weeks unless the man sees himself and his country as being insulted and injured. We have not been doing well for most of the past year or two in Mexico, Central, and South America. Street riots with all blame going our way, will be very damaging, and heaven help us if some overwrought maniac sets off a keg of explosives and gets the whole world involved;"

"It more than irks me to be domineered by that two-bit crook. I know Ivory White; he is a fine American, a good and loyal help to this administration; and, I will not remain patient forever, mark my word."

The word seeped out to people in the administration who matter—one of whom was Sybil Norcroft, the DCIA with ice water for blood. Shortly after she got the message from the president, she got a call from her old friend, JPAMJ McGee.

"Security office, to whom may direct your call, Sir?" Sybil's ever watchful secretary answered when McGee's call came in.

"This is McGee. Please put me through to DCIA Norcroft."

"May I tell the director what the call is about?"

"Tell her it's about Mexico; that should suffice."

"I'll try, but she is very busy, as you might imagine."

"I will appreciate your effort, Ma'am."

Sybil was on the line forty-five seconds later, "Hope you weren't kept too long, McGee," she said, "my day was spoiled by some regular spy stuff. What's up in your world... which seems to be converging with mine with some regularity."

"It does seem so. This time, a good American, and a mutual friend of ours, is very unjustly being detained in some hellhole of a Mexican prison on trumped up human trafficking charges."

"You mean you think Ivory White is not an international and well-known trafficker of human beings?"

He laughed.

"Look Sybil, we need to tap a few of your resources to begin working on an escape from the prison. If "Joaquín Archivaldo "El Chapo" Guzmán Loera, can do it; so, can we. But I really have more in mind to share information with the Mexican president that he might not like to be made public and in fact would rather make a little trade for with us for the release of Ivory.

Dirt is what we need, and we need it soon, my friend. Ivory does not deserve such treatment, but President Juan Diego Sanchez-Porteño certainly does. I think that is Sanchez-Porteño's Achilles heel, and knowledge of it is our leverage. Let's get details and move against him as quickly as possible."

It was evident to Caitlin and McGee that the foot dragging of government was not the only way to go. Their partner was likely to be suffering considerably in the corrupt jail system of the corrupt Mexican President Juan Diego Sanchez-Porteño, and his equally unscrupulous cronies who were making fortunes off human trafficking. MacGee and Caitlin parlayed with Chief Inspector Miguel de Pasos-Vásquez about how to get the most telling dirt on his not particularly beloved current president. They met at the theater where *The Man from La Mancha* was playing, and the policeman was playing the title role. After the curtain closed, and the audience made their exit, McGee and Caitlin walked to the park.

de Pasos-Vásquez stepped out of the shadows.

"You know that what you are asking could get all of us killed," he said as his greeting.

"Or, it could get Ivory saved and you promoted to chief of police, and after that, maybe a change to a political career and take the presidency from that vile Juan Diego Sanchez-Porteño who thinks he is untouchable."

"Brave words. Let's see what we can do working from the shadows," de Pasos-Vásquez said.

Ivory had bruises on top of his bruises. His skin retained only limited areas of his original ebony color; now most of him was purple from the daily beatings. On the seventh day in a row, his cell door opened abruptly with a clang as it always did to initiate another beating by causing a startle reaction and fear. It was part of the brutal ritual, and Ivory had not become accustomed to it—not by a long shot.

What was different this morning was that the head of the squad of thugs was a different man, an Anglo with prison tattoos, two scars on his face, a bent nose, and cauliflower ears.

"You comink wit me," the new man said. "I got somethink special in store for you today."

He turned to his four-man squad and said, "I take care of this today. Warden has something special for me to do and a message to send him. You go take a hour siesta."

Nobody turns down the chance for an extracurricular siesta, and it was no sooner said than done.

As soon as the cell door closed behind him, the new man stepped close to Ivory's right side and whispered into his ear, "Don' talk. Leesen. Maybe bugs in here. Here is message from warden. I am a prisoner like you. But I get some special privileges for doing certain things. You heard of Joaquín Archivaldo Guzmán Loera commonly known as "El Chapo"—"shorty"–because he was only 5'6"?

Ivory shrugged. He had heard something about an escape in Mexico; but, since it was in Mexico—a place he could care less about–he had never paid attention to the details; and it showed on his face.

"I will give you the short talk. El Chapo was a *Mexican* former *drug lord* and former leader of the Sinaloa Cartel, a big international crime syndicate. He was the most powerful drug trafficker in the world for a long time. He escaped prior to formal sentencing in 2015, through a tunnel under his jail cell. That cell was right here in this same prison, *Amigo*."

The light was beginning to come on in Ivory's mind, but he said nothing, just listened with enough interest for the warden's man to continue.

"On July 11, 2015, Guzmán escaped from theese very prison. The shower area was the only part of his cell that was not visible through the security camera. After the guards did not see him for twenty-five minutes on surveillance video, they went looking for him. When they reached his cell, our star inmate was gone. It was queekly discovered he had escaped through a tunnel leading from the shower area to a house construction site about a mile away in a Santa Juanita neighborhood.

The tunnel lay 33 feet deep underground, and Guzmán had used a ladder to climb to the bottom. The tunnel that barely accommodated Guzmán was 5 ft. 7 in. tall and 30 in. in width. It was equipped with artificial light, air ducts, and high-quality construction materials. In addition, an amazingly designed motorcycle was found in the tunnel, which authorities think was used to transport materials for construction as well as Guzmán himself."

"Interesting story, '*Amigo*', but what does this have to do with me?" Ivory asked dubiously.

CHAPTER
TWO

President Willets asked DCIA Sybil Norcroft to head up a secret task force to get Ivory White out of the Mexican prison and to bring down the profoundly corrupt Mexican president, Juan Diego Sanchez-Porteño, who was ruining everything the US was doing to interdict illicit drug traffic and now human trafficking. It was repugnant to him and somehow strangely personal.

"We are not going to get anywhere following the rule of law. Sanchez-Porteño is the law, and he plays only by his rules. Sybil, you are very good at playing outside the prescribed lines; and you have some unsavory friends whom I greatly admire. Bring them in. We will all deny their existence of course. There is plenty of money for this mission, don't worry about that; just don't get caught and make me ask, 'Sybil who?' Keep me posted through Dick Weatherly in the ODNI—all encrypted with rotating passwords–that kind of cloak-and-dagger stuff–I don't want to know about."

Sybil simply nodded her understanding and left the Oval Office without speaking to be sure nothing she said was recorded. As soon as she got back to her seventh-floor office at Langley, she got hold of her black-ops specialists, Lincoln Howard and Mac Young.

Her secretary connected with Lincoln first, "I am calling for your favorite lady friend. Are you on a secure line? I am."

"What does the Snow Queen need, my other lady friend?"

"To talk to you and Mac Young, Is now a good time?"

"I'll make it a good time."

"Give me five minutes, please."

The DCIA was on the line in three minutes, "Hi, Lincoln, how're things going?"

"Busy, as you well know. I take it this is more important."

"If you can get your number two to handle your other work, then, yes, it is."

"We're pretty much mopping up, and it is actually a pretty good time. Give me the news."

"Top Secret, eyes and ears only for POTUS, DNI, me, and your unit. Mexico is the place, and jail break for a VIPI is the first op, and the second op is a large-scale disinformation program. The target is Mexican President Juan Diego Sanchez-Porteño. This is going to be a long talk, and the operation will take a while. I'll get Mac on the line; so, I don't have to present it twice."

"Good. I'll hang on the line. Everything okay on your end?"

"Peachy."

It took thirty minutes to connect Mac into a conference call with all the security apparati in place.

"Okay, I'll be brief," Sybil said as soon as both Lincoln and Mac were on the line. She told them of the international delicacy, the importance of getting Ivory White back as intact as possible, and of the general basics of her plan.

Her last instruction was for them to include McGee and Associates in the planning and execution of plans because they had a dog in the fight, and because they knew guys who knew guys; and they knew how to keep their lips zipped.

Mac happened to run into McGee on Fifth Avenue by coincidence the very next day and engaged him in conversation.

The salient parts of the communication were these: after the introduction and brief chat about the Mets and the news about secession by several states going through the federal judicial system, "We have a mutual lady friend with ice in her veins instead of blood. She wants a favor, a big one. Are we on the same page?"

"I think so. What's up?"

"Mac... that's my name, and my friend Lincoln is involved."

"Serious, secret, and dangerous, I gather, with the two of you and her ladyship taking part in a Byzantine plot."

"Well, I'm just a blue-collar kind of guy, and I wouldn't use such university sort of words, but yeah, it's a typical mess coming from Virginia."

They agreed to meet on Monday in Del Rio, Texas in Benny's Café on 650 South Main Street for breakfast. It was less than five miles and twenty minutes to Cuidad de Acuña, Mexico with even the heaviest traffic Del Rio ever experienced They also agreed to include Caitlin O'Brian and two of her unusual friends, as well as "technicians and mechanics" from the Company for which Mac worked.

In the sinister and brutal confines of Altiplano maximum security prison in Almoloya de Juarez, west of Mexico City, Ivory White and Donald Gutiérrez–the trustee guard–had gotten far enough towards trusting one another that they had exchanged names, the minimum of useful information about each other; and–most important–what Gutiérrez had in mind. Ivory was still not entirely trusting; he never was with anyone but McGee and Caitlin. But he was impressed with Gutiérrez's wealth of information, his experience in the prison, and his overall plan for an escape from the pit of hell in which they both resided. The risks were colossally high, but the rewards—getting out of Altiplano—were worth almost any risk.

Reporters working for President Sanchez-Porteño, and his lacky–the prison commandant–had leaked photos out to the entire world showing how brutally "fellow prisoners" had treated the American Black man. When questioned by reporters from the *Washington Post, New York Times*, and the Del Rio *830 Times*, the arrogant president agreed only to the reporters getting one statement for publication.

"It is regrettable that anyone in our penal system should be treated so badly. However, we are not rich country like the United States, and we cannot afford very expensive country club security updates. Also, I would ask, what do you really expect from common criminals—choir boy behavior? There are dangerous criminals in our jails, some from the United States."

His point having been made, Sanchez-Porteño had bigger fish to fry, such as finding ever more complex and devious ways to launder the constantly increasing income coming in to his personal coffers—including dirty money from those ever-faithful human traffickers—and the reliable marijuana smugglers. It was vexing; but, then, such are the problems of growing rich in a poor country with a limited education. He and his commandant generally ignored Ivory White, and the beatings stopped for lack of a useful purpose.

Meetings with Ivory and Donald Gutiérrez became infrequent, more important, and less subtle.

After three months of no more corporal punishment, Ivory was released into the general population; and he and Gutiérrez began to talk turkey about details of planning an escape.

Breakfast at Benny's Café was a hometown mixture of very generous helpings of Tex-Mex breakfast omelet, bean chilaquiles with avocado and *queso fresco*, and common American breakfast staples including Aunt Jemima's white flour pancakes, spam, extra fat milk, capsaicin heat, and quick, productive, planning, for the upcoming disinformation program that was projected to begin that week in Mexico.

Caitlin was the acknowledged best ad writer and the most creative and believable liar; so, she agreed to head-up the creative end of the group's efforts. She was also assigned—along with one or the other of the

Richter twins—to come up with any dirt they could dig up about Sanchez-Porteño. Because each of the twins was considered to be native fluent in Spanish–including Mexican slanguage–they were tasked to communicate the disinformation necessary for the Spanish speaking president and his cronies. It required a very good rolling conversation to the new president and his benefitting friends, and weavers of convincingly tantalizing get-rich quick schemes that operated the old-fashioned way—a combination of flattery, promises of untold wealth beyond even his previously impressive scams, leverage against new construction and buildings to extort from them as much as the market would bear, extortion rackets with him as the silent partner, all free of risk.

Underlings received arm twisting, supposedly ordered by the esteemed president of the country. Everyone received the benefit of the CIA's remarkable auditory and visual recording for posterity and for President Willet's personal uses in dealing with carefully chosen Mexicans. Sybil contributed the linguistic skills learned from the take-down of the populist British prime minister and despot to create eminently believable professional videos of the president meeting in smoke filled back rooms with the worst of the worst criminals. The technicians in her employ created made for TV high definition, superb acoustics, and excellent lighting technology, to produce several very credible scenarios which implicated the photogenic president. Without a team of professional university applied linguistic experts, it was not possible to detect that speech had been put in President Sanchez-

Porteño's mouth; his mouth movements synchronized with his contrived utterances; and his facial expressions were in perfect agreement with his emphases, emotions, and speech and movement patterns, all created by a computer.

Given the amount of video material available to the linguistic sciences professionals from his huge archive of speeches and casual conversations recorded by FBI, CIA, and reporters', sources, it was not particularly difficult. Caitlin met with Chief Inspector Miguel de Pasos-Vásquez after she had reviewed the phony incriminating videos with her favorite male star, the Mexican president and pronounced them as impossible to differentiate from speeches that could very well have come from the esteemed president's very brain and mouth.

She and de Pasos-Vásquez spent several trying hours trying to debunk the videos.

"So, Chief Inspector, do you find any lack of synchrony of the man's lips and his spoken words anywhere?"

"I don't, and believe you me, I tried as hard as I could. My life and career depends on being right."

"How about the content; did it seem like Sanchez-Porteño's kind of thinking, his little quirks of speech, his ways of stressing one thing and minimizing another as he talks?"

"If I didn't know you had created these scenarios on a computer because you told me so, I would never have tumbled to any of them being fake... not even a single word, thought, or paragraph. They are fantastically good. I have to ask how they are going to be used?"

"You and I will act as advisors; but the US president, DCIA Norcroft, and my boss, McGee, will create a situation where the incriminating true-to-life videos will just happen to appear while he is giving some phony appeal for help for the poor children, or for starting another 'War on Police Corruption' or the like. Mark my word, Chief, it will be when thousands or hundreds of thousands are gathered to hear and see the man; and the Mexican and world press is gathered to report his every idea.

"They love to see him, hear him, and hate him; but he is good fodder for news and laughs around the office water cooler. No matter what he says after that, his career goose will be cooked. Maybe there will be a war to decide the next crook to be president; or, maybe, someone will be brought forward to be a statesman and change Mexico's path into the future. Who could that possibly be?"

Chief Inspector de Pasos-Vásquez drew his fingers across his lips to sign 'silence' by crossing his flat, open hands part way across his lips then released them by putting his index finger vertically across his lips in the universal 'shhh' sign for "quiet".

CHAPTER
THREE

I t had been three weeks since Ivory and Donald Gutiérrez had met even in passing. That reduced Ivory's tension, but it did not improve his need for hoping. The beatings had stopped; now, Ivory received only the occasional back slap across the face or kick in his sensitive lateral thighs, enough to keep multi-colored bruises in constant rainbow flowering. He was now no different than anyone else in the general population and had no more knowledge about what was going on the outside world or hope for the future than any of them did. Ivory realized that his attitude of acceptance was unhealthy for working towards his own future, and especially so because he was beginning to be a reasonably well-behaved con… a lifer.

A bit of improvement occurred in his dull routine life on the Monday when his fourth month of incarceration began. A different trusty than Gutiérrez walked along the opposite direction of the long single line of inmates marching to six a.m. *desayuno*. He was walking with the warden on the officer's left to provide a buffer between the warden and the unpredictable violent men in the breakfast line. He leaned slightly out of line so that his right shoulder bumped Ivory's right side.

The trusty stopped, turned, growled, then whispered, "Gutiérrez, tonight center place…" then he said loudly, "*hijo de puta*" [the '*puta*' being an abbreviation of *prostituta*].

No one but Ivory paid any attention to the encounter. The trusty's reference to the "center place" meant only one thing, the double poles in the exact center of the exercise yard where prisoner whippings were conducted. It was a place of foreboding and superstition for almost every inmate. The poles were set in concrete and rocks were caulked into place to form a very rough support for the poles and a rough, sharp, surface for the inmates' bare–and often beaten–foot soles to endure. It was a favorite place for prisoner clandestine meetings because of the shadows cast by the punishment structure in the moonlight.

Ivory did not expect much, since little had happened in his previous brief encounters with the head trusty. It was not as if he had a busy shedule, however; so, he planned his exit from his cell and his clandestine round-about route to where the whipping posts menaced the exercise yard, making certain that he could get there in the expected deep darkness.

Supper was beans and rice as opposed to the rice and beans that made up the *desayuno*. As an added treat the cons were served a hunk of week-old bread which was just developing a grey velvety fuzz of mold. Everyone was hungry enough to scrape off the added bit of nature provided by the prison cooks.

It had been too hot during the day for any fights to take place; so, it was a particularly boring way to pass the hours before midnight. He sat on his cot and tried to force himself to read another chapter of *Cien Años de Soledad*, [*A Hundred years of Solitude*] by the Colombian, Gabriel García Márquez. It was in nearly new condition despite having been received at the prison shortly after it was written in the 1960s. Ivory presumed that the pristine condition of the famous book could be attributed to the fact that it was more than twenty pages long, had no pictures, was not pornographic, and used multi-syllabic words—none of which suited the generally minimal literacy of the prison population, including the guards and the warden.

He asked for and received permission from the night shift guard for a twenty-minute break to go outside and get a bit of the evening cool air. It cost him eighty pesos—roughly four US dollars—from the stash that McGee had had smuggled in. His cache was getting smaller by the day.

He hugged the east wall of the cell bloc and stayed in the shadows until he saw the whipping posts directly west of him in the center of the yard. There were no people to be seen or heard anywhere. It crossed his mind that this could be a set-up for getting him thrown into solitary or shanked just to annoy the American government.

He had to put that out of his mind in order to concentrate. His adrenalin levels were set for fight or flight, and every nerve was atingle with hot intensity as he crawled on all fours out into the relative light away from the prison bloc walls. Once out in the yard, he did a quick commando crawl in the prone position. He looked over his shoulders frequently and froze in position at even the movement of the tiny breezes wafting across him.

Ivory hardly took a breath until he reached the relative safety of the rock piles holding up the heavy vertical whipping posts. His eyes had adjusted well to the darkness, and he saw what looked like a pile of prison clothes lying in the darkest area of shadow.

"Donald, that you to my left?"

There was no answer for a full minute.

Then, "*Si, Amigo*. Is Donald."

"We don't have much time. Why this meeting?"

"Good news and something of a plan."

"Sounds something short of a perfect opportunity."

"The warden and some big shots have planned a big party *aqui* for some grandees to celebrate the *Dia de la Independencia* on September 16."

"I have lost all track of the dates and even which day of the week today is. Tell me about this celebration."

"Oh, I forget that ju are jus a Gringo. This is the day when Padre Don Miguel Gregorio Antonio Francisco Ignacio Hidalgo-Costilla y Gallaga Mandarte Villaseñor, more commonly known by us little people as Don Miguel Hidalgo y Costilla, *el padre de la nacione*, started the War of Independence from the accursed Spanish. Eet was 1810, I think. The day is one of the major holidays in Mexico, one of the *días de asueto* or statutory holidays. Big fuss over it, and the warden wants to show off how modern and kind Altiplano maximum security prison in Almoloya de Juarez, really is."

Gutiérrez said it with an appropriately disdainful sneer. "I'm listening," Ivory said.

"I have to make it quick. We cannot take any chances of being caught together or of breaking any rules. Just listen and do as I say, and I think ju and me can get out of this hellhole one day. Here's the deal, Amigo."

DCIA Sybil Norcroft arranged for her most trusted agents, Mac Young and Lincoln Howard, to rendezvous with Caitlin O'Brien and McGee in Mexico DF. The place chosen was an obscure hole-in-the-wall café on Peralvillo 30, Cuauhtémoc in the Tepito neighborhood of Mexico City—the black market of the capital city. Nice people did not go to Tepito, and most such people had never heard of the Correo Español Café or it's dicey reputation. Known as the "*Barrio Bravo*" by the locals, Tepito is essentially a huge outdoor market that is especially busy on Sundays, when the neighboring *Lagunilla* [outdoor] market is also in full swing. Tapito is one part of the larger *colonía* Morelos, and the entire section of Mexico DF has a reputation for crime and piracy.

The CIA related assemblage entered the eating place in separate small groups, including three thuggish looking brutes who served as the muscle for the group. Caitlin was the only female, and she looked as if she belonged. Small as she was, Caitlin's martial arts training and proficiency always made her seem to be the least likely person in a bar to be molested by oversexed lotharios. There was just something about the girl.

The dining area was filled with smoke and the odors of Sangria and marijuana. Visibility was well below par;

and by safety convention, no one looked at anyone else. The Company group slowly gathered in a back room, and the Italian-Portuguese waiter closed the door. There was little talking when the waiter was in the room. He suggested the house specialties, *cabrito* [roasted goat], *paella valenciana*, and several offerings of *la comida michoacana*—including *consomé de birria*, and a *molcajete* [a mortar made of volcanic stone filled with grilled meats, cheese, and roasted *nopales*].

The food and the sangria were good, and little was said until after the desserts of flan, *crema castalana, turron, yemas,* and *polvoron.*

Mac was the senior of the two CIA agents, and he spoke first.

"We have the tools to bring down Juan Diego Sanchez-Porteño; or, more accurately to have his own people do it. We have to be very careful how we proceed from here on out. No one can ever know that this came from the United States. No one can ever find out that the images and messages we scatter around are the work of genius fakers. None of us will survive a leak or an expose, and it is a certainty that our friend, Ivory White, will suffer the most of any of us. Our president will be humiliated, and the rewards for Sanchez-Porteño will be to make him all but untouchable if we screw this up.

"We talked for a long time with the DCIA and hatched a plan that will make Sanchez-Porteño's exposure complete and like an atom bomb went off while he was sitting on the crapper. So, listen very carefully."

A month before the day, the prison came alive with preparations for the huge celebration for the *Dia de la Independencia* on September 16 slated to take place in—of all places—the hard-time Altiplano maximum security prison, Almoloya de Juarez. Truck loads of bunting, national, and province flags, banners, and streamers, moved into the exercise yard; and trustees worked for two days to cover the grim whipping posts center landmark of the prison. The dirt ground of the exercise area was being replaced with enough synthetic grass cover to make it look almost verdant.

Ivory and Donald were ordered to help set up the folding chairs and the speakers' dais. Obviously, many hundreds of people were expected to see what a prison was really like and to hear from the famous president of Mexico. If nothing else took place, Ivory enjoyed the time out of his cell and to do some useful work for a rare change in the mind-numbing routine.

Three months prior to the day, Sybil Norcroft, McGee, and Mexican Chief Inspector Miguel de Pasos-Vásquez, gathered in San Diego, California to visit a "friend" who was incarcerated in the prison there. *Jose Sanchez-Villalobos*–the tunnel mastermind behind El Chapo's underground smuggling routes–had been arrested and extradited to the United States after the capture of El Chapo and his turning state's evidence in return for a less harsh imprisonment in the US. Sanchez-Villalobos was placed in the San Diego, California RJDCF [Richard J. Donovan Correctional Facility] for much the same reason.

RJDCF's primary mission was to provide housing for General Population and SNY [Sensitive Needs Yard], Level I, II, III, & IV, inmates serving their term of incarceration at RJDCF. He was placed in the level IV facility to protect him from the gangs who were after him to prevent him from giving up sensitive gang information to the US feds.

He was by far the most protected prisoner in the entire United States corrections system at any level or in any place. He was remanded to the custody of the California Department of Corrections and Rehabilitations like all inmates; but due to safety concerns, he was separated from General Population inmates to serve his term of incarceration—life in prison without parole. Like the other SNY inmates, Sanchez-Villalobos was given the opportunity to work and attend education programs such as college courses, Career Technical Education–carpentry, welding, electronics, and building maintenance–and to participate in inmate work labor outside the walls of the SNY facility with supervision.

The politically correct mission statement expressed this as the opportunity for self-improvement.

The CIA agents hung up as McGee expected they would, and he immediately made flight reservations for himself and Caitlin, first class to San Diego's Brown Field Municipal Airport [airport code SDM] in the Otay Mesa neighborhood of San Diego 13 miles southeast of downtown San Diego. The field was named in honor of Commander Melville S. Brown, USN, who was killed in an airplane crash in 1936. The next stop was Tijuana

International Airport located approximately 3.3 miles northeast of Tijuana and 16 miles from San Diego.

McGee thought it wise to avoid any recordable involvement with San Diego proper. The customs documents were taken care of in flight, and the stamp in their passports was all the American citizens needed to enter Mexico and transfer back to the United States post mission—a circuitous route linked to spycraft. The automobile trip from Tijuana back to San Diego took an hour, including passing through customs, and negotiating the light traffic on that off day for tourists. They had a nondescript rental car and parked it in a far corner of the zoo parking lot in Balboa Park.

Both McGee and Caitlin knew the two CIA officers, Mac and Lincoln, on sight, and were also coaxed into the correct meeting spot by seeing the two tough guys holding root beer floats.

CHAPTER
FOUR

D onald Gutiérrez and Ivory White made sure their association was not entirely evident to the other inmates and the guards or other staff. Most of their time together was at night or in what appeared to be casual encounters. Several times each day, the two would make themselves scarce and would meet near the old cell where Joaquín Archivaldo "El Chapo" Guzmán Loera had been housed during his confinement in the Almoloya de Juarez prison. No effort was made to keep prisoners or anyone else from seeing the cell or the bathtub under which was the famous escape tunnel entrance. There was a circle of yellow crime scene tape around it which did nothing to impede the curious onlooker. Every afternoon and every evening they could, Donald and Ivory sneaked into the cell block and worked in the tunnel to dismantle the debris purposely placed there to keep would-be escapees from making progress.

One of the two men kept watch while the other worked. It was ponderously slow work owing to the need for silence and avoiding suspicion. Nevertheless, the tunnel entrance was cleared enough to allow a man to enter and crawl or squat walk about ten feet. The debris collection was becoming less formidable as the work advanced.

"How long do you think it will take before we break through into open tunnel all the way to Tijuana, Donald?" Ivory asked after two exhausting weeks of effort.

"Four guys worked about two weeks piling stuff inside. They were day laborers supplemented by trustees; so, you know nobody was in any hurry to get the job done. They were paid by the hour, and it was hot and dusty in there."

"That would mean that we are close to breaking through, doesn't it?"

"Yeah, but it's not done until it's done. We just have to keep on picking our way at the pile and finding places to put the lumber we bring out. Be patient, Amigo. *Con paciencia.*"

"And no mistakes. I've heard it before. But it is difficult and nerve wracking."

It was September the first, and Ivory could not help but having Matthew Arnold's timeless poem intrude on his psyche, *"But at my back I always hear Time's wingèd chariot hurrying near; And yonder all before us lie Deserts of vast eternity."*

The meeting of McGee and Caitlin with the two veteran spies, Mac and Lincoln, was entirely functional and to the point.

"This is what we have to accomplish," Mac said, stating the obvious, "Ivory won't last forever in there, and means of escape are few and far between. We act now or maybe we'll never see another opportunity."

"So, we *carpe diem* or wait for our friend to wither and die and for the US to suffer ongoing humiliation at the discretion of the Crook in Charge in Mexico," Caitlin said emphasizing hers and MacGees' agreement.

"So far as we can see, that's pretty much all there is. The politician's and even the Company's ideas are too slow and too complicated. They depend on Sanchez-Porteño developing a sense of shame or even a conscience because of the DCIA's clever campaign to get the man to recognize that by selecting the USA as an enemy, it will go badly for him in the long run."

"And, we really don't have a long run. We have got to get Ivory out of there."

Lincoln surprised McGee and Caitlin with a revelation.

"Only us and a few of Director Norcroft's select wizards know what I am about to tell you. They have all but perfected a scenario in which they hijack Sanchez-Porteño's speech in the prison on September the sixteenth and show him as a criminal in league with traffickers and a co-criminal in an ongoing criminal conspiracy with the Mexican cartels and the Mafia in the US. They have created a movie with some special effects by linguists to put words in the man's mouth that will bring him down. They hope and believe that he will fall from the revelations and his successors will take down his system of corruption, especially in the military, law enforcement, and government, and will clean up the prison system; so, our friend, Ivory White, can be released, and his record expunged."

"No matter how good that clever ploy is, it is unlikely to happen quickly enough to save Ivory. We have to be the boots on the ground to make that happen," Caitlin said earnestly.

"Not quite so, Caitlin," Lincoln said. "As we speak, Director Norcroft of the CIA, Director of the FBI Landon Murphy, Mexican Chief Inspector Miguel de Pasos-Vásquez, and the president of the US, have all signed off on her caper; and the man previously languishing in the prison, Sinaloa cartel drug tunneler and trafficker Jose Sanchez-Villalobos "Lord of the Tunnels", aka *Nariz* or "Nose", Sanchez-Villalobos, has been released and is busy at work opening his previous tunnel from Tijuana to Almoloya de Juarez prison, and creating another to put Mexican law enforcement off the scent.

Villalobos has real incentive: if he finishes the new tunneling job in time to get Ivory out safely, the life sentence for *"Nariz"* is going to be shortened to two years... maybe with time off for good behavior. If he fails, the Snow Queen, and her cohorts won't like the criminal mastermind so much, and who knows what grief he could come to?"

McGee said, "The lady is somethin' else. She has bigger cojones that a dozen sailors who have been six months at sea!"

With two days to go before *El Dia de la Independencia*, Ivory and Donald moved the last crude barrier of 2 X 4s blocking the way into the main tunnel to freedom. They were soaked in sweat and exhausted having lost two nights' sleep getting the job done. They were fully aware of the bright side of the equation: freedom was only a mile and a brisk walk away. So far as they could tell; no one but them knew of the reopening of Villalobos's tunnel; and the diversion by President Sanchez-Porteño's grandiose speech was very nearly perfect. Now, if they could only stay in their cells and hold their breath for two days.

McGee, Caitlin, Chief Inspector Miguel de Pasos-Vásquez, joined Sanchez-Villalobos and his select crew of tunnelers—who owed their status as rich men and free—to the "Nariz" in getting the entire length of the original tunnel open, electric light and aeration system operational, new sets of clothes and identities for the two escapees designed and delivered to the prison end of the tunnel; and post-escape transportation to the US border finalized. DCIA Norcroft took responsibility for getting the two men new and authentic identities to get across the border.

President Willets asked the ingenious and resourceful director of the Puzzle Palace, how she managed to do that.

Sybil answered laconically, "I know a guy."

Sanchez-Villalobos was a hard task-master and did not permit any of his workmen a second chance if or when they made mistakes. Half of the criminal population of Tijuana revolved through the tunneling crew before the project was completed. Of necessity, he had to grant a little latitude for McGee, Caitlin, the two obvious spies, and the Chief Inspector from Mexico whom he knew personally, and who he hoped to be able to form a mutually beneficial relationship after the dust settled; and he was able to get back to his chosen profession.

The criminal was a mastermind in several avenues of his tunnel building profession. He knew how to get the most work out of a tunnel worker, supply chain expert, explosives technician, and an accountant. He was a master at organizing criminals into effective enterprises, and he did not need a calculator to do his necessary math. He was a master of men—even lords of the crime world—because he could outthink, out maneuver, and could come up with plans that would have stupefied a lesser man. He was not afraid to get dirt on his hands, or blood. He had seen plenty of both in his career. He was not a dandy, suave, debonair, or handsome. But he was charismatic, and both men and women admired him for his industry, his natural power, and his chutzpah.

The Americans moved aside as the work progressed. It was going faster and farther than any of them could have imagined. It began to look as if he would be able to open the original tunnel and use it to his advantage to get to a point where he could start a secret diversion tunnel to get to the jail cell of El Chapo, the last place where anyone would have thought an escape could be brought off again.

McGee was twenty yards into the obtuse angle of the diversionary tunnel when he and a Nahua Indian miner from Ixtacamaxtitlan, Mexico with twenty years of experience, ran into a serious surprise. Water began to trickle from a fissure in the rock, then it burbled out in a steady stream.

"*Painal... yoliliztli... motlaloa*!!!" the little man screamed. He looked back at McGee as he ran and realized that the city man did not understand the sacred Aztec language

[Nahuatl]; so, he switched quickly to Spanish, "*Corre por tu vida, date prisa!*" [run for your life, hurry!].

McGee got that and turned and ran as fast as his tired legs and back could manage. Behind him a torrent of murky wáter four feet in diameter gushed out of what was a fissure that was barely thicker than a piece of paper a momento ago. Ahead of him, the Nahua and McGee screamed at the other workers to run for the exit, or stand aside.

The water began to fill the main tunnel. Shovels, picks, cell phones, coffee cups, and packs of cigarettes, began to fall from frightened hands as the pell mell rush to escape gathered strength. It was nearly a run of half a mile, and after ten to fifteen minutes, the terrified workmen and women were struggling to waddle along through foot deep water and rising.

At the mouth of the tunnel, the depth of the water lessened as the width of the stream spread out. The strongest of the men hurried back into the tunnel to help the stragglers. The water continued to flow for hours but lessened in total output until it was safe to return to work.

Sanchez-Villalobos was soaked from head to foot but kept on straining to pull workers and equipment out; so, they could begin again as soon as it was even barely safe.

"Hurry up. We have to get back in. The water was just an inconvenience. We will work even harder now to save our *compatriotas.*"

Not one to shirk himself, the ex-con rushed back into the tunnel leading workers rather than pushing them from behind. Now, the floor was mud three inches deep, and the work had become incredibly filthy, making it difficult to see the way, to walk without falling, and to find solid rock to chop at. Sanchez-Villalobos was loathe to use explosives for fear of opening another underground cistern and killing off his best workers.

An hour later, the water dried up, and the tunnel became insufferably hot. The periods of work alternated with periods of drinking water and resting in the fresh air at the mouth of the tunnel.

McGee asked the tunnel master, "Should we get more workmen? This is too slow a process."

"Si," Sanchez-Villalobos answered grinding his teeth and cursing God and the elements of nature.

He gave McGee a backhanded wave, and the New York PI rushed to the opening where he could get cell reception and began making calls to anyone and everyone he knew in Mexico and Guatemala to find miners. He arranged for helicopters and fixed-wing planes of all kinds to provide new workers. He promised the sun, the moon, and the stars, throwing fiscal discretion to the winds.

His work paid off. In three hours, the first plane load of miners disembarked, dressed and ready for work. They entered the queue of men and the rhythm of the work and rest cycle. Trucks brought in water and ice to hydrate and cool the miners. Work began to pick up.

Sanchez-Villalobos found McGee.

"Young man," he said, which made McGee laugh, "we need something like five hundred wheelbarrows to push the debris out of our way and get the lines of workers moving faster. I estimate that we have something like three hundred yards to go, and three days to do it. We need a miracle."

"I'll get you one.

He called Chief Inspector Miguel de Pasos-Vásquez for assistance.

"Miguel, this is McGee. We have run into a couple of problems. We are fighting mud, heat, and water, and now the mining debris is collecting to a degree that we can't get past each other to keep the work going. We have less than three days to finish this, or it will all have been for nothing. Can you get two or three hundred wheelbarrows?"

de Pasos-Vásquez hesitated only a moment.

"I can. I will get hold of the district commanders of the police forces and the military I know I can trust. I can go one better than your ask; I think I can get men to man the barrows once I can convey to them that is about bringing down Sanchez-Porteño."

"How about security? Won't someone blab, and bring the president and his crooks in the military and police forces down on us?"

"This will be a test of my reputation and of the men's belief in the quality of my character. I will be staking my life on the outcome."

"*And mine*," McGee said to himself silently.

CHAPTER
FIVE

As he had done as a tunneler for the drug lords, Sanchez-Villalobos thought it prudent to create a safety tunnel, an extra one that only a very few chosen builders and financiers knew about. When he worked for El Chapo, José Sánchez Villalobos was the brains behind two state-of-the-art and highly profitable tunnels linking Tijuana on the Mexican side and San Diego on the U.S. side. He was quite proud of his accomplishment even though it eventually led to his downfall, his sentence to a lifetime in prison without the possibility of parole. He approached the SAC in San Diego and made a proposition.

"Special Agent Dastrup, I won't waste your time or mine. We are both very busy and have deadlines to keep. First, I report that our tunnel construction is going well. We will finish in two days, three tops. I have a sneaking suspicion that everything is going too well. We have not seen a cop the entire time we have been working, and it is a suspension of judgment beyond what any rational person would consider plausible. I am becoming more and more of the opinion that it is intended for us to succeed in getting your Ivory White person out of the prison and into the El Chapo's tunnel without any serious interference by prison or police officers."

"Why in the world would the corrupt cops or military or government officers want to do that? The very next day, the news outlets would show photos of the lot of them with egg on their faces. I can just see the headlines now: 'BUNGLERS AT SUPER MAX MEXICAN PRISON ALLOW ANOTHER HIGH-PROFILE PRISONER TO ESCAPE! American gangster, Ivory White, escapes through the same tunnel as El Chapo. Baffled Leaders from president to the beat cop do not have a clue.'"

"Ah, Señor SAC, think for a moment. What if the headlines were different… something like: FOOLS BUNGLE MAJOR ATTEMPT BY AMERICANS TO HAVE THEIR SPY/CRIMINAL CIA DRUG LORD ESCAPE FROM ALTIPLANO PRISON IN JUAREZ. Criminal identified as Ivory White, a known drug and human trafficker, fell into a clever trap set by President Sanchez-Porteño. Several American operatives and corrupt Mexican Policemen, including Chief Inspector Miguel de Pasos-Vásquez taken in the trap and humiliated.'"

SAC Dastrup had no comeback.

"That's a terrible thought, Señor Villalobos. Any ideas about how to avoid that calamity?"

"Oh, *Si*, Señor. It will take a great deal of money and the US federal government's convincing of the New York

City Sand Hogs to come on board to get my plan done on time and safely."

"I'm listening, but you nearly lost me when you said, 'a great deal of money'. This had better be good."

Thus, was hatched the audacious engineering plan to dig a secret alternative tunnel with El Chapo and Villalobos's original tunnel used as a stalking horse.

President Willets telephoned New York Mayor Walter Stephens on his secure line:

"Walter, this is President Willets. I presume this is a fully secure line. Is that correct?"

"Yes, Mr. President, it is. Your security chief and his technologists came to my office this morning and made sure. What's up?"

"We need your help to save a good New Yorker, a man you have had occasion to get to know. He is Ivory White, one of McGee's associates."

"Everybody knows about him, Sir. He is a fall guy locked up in one of those God forsaken Mexican hellhole jails because he and his people humiliated the great president of the country over one of his corruption enterprises. That about right?"

"On the nail."

"I would be glad to help. What do you want me to do?"

"Lester Adkins is a member of the other party from me and is not likely to cooperate, but I need the full and silent help of his Laborers' Local Union 147. I know you have a fairly civil—if not exactly cordial—relationship with him and his guys. Here's what I want them to do, and to do it instead of anything else they may be doing under your great city for the moment."

New York Local 147 members are the city's tunnel diggers who are of largely Irish immigrant extraction and have worked on the underground infrastructure of the great city since the 1872. The Sandhogs started working on the Brooklyn Bridge and have worked on such projects ever since, including the Lincoln, Holland, Queens-Midtown, New York to New Jersey, and Brooklyn-Battery Tunnels, and on with most of New York City's subways, waterways, and sewers. They are indispensable to the city and the region, and they have a sense of pride that goes with it.

As soon as the president hung up, Mayor Stephens put in a call to 4332 Katonah Avenue in the Bronx. Having been born and raised on Kayppock Street in Speight den Duyvil half a block from the old 50th Precinct house, the mayor knew the area well and also its denizens. His old Dutch neighborhood was located at the confluence of the Harlem and Hudson Rivers under the Henry Hudson Bridge. Various names for the area used by those fond of it and not so much were the Spike and Devil, Spitting Devil, Spilling Devil, Spiten Debill, and Spouting Devil. The Irish—who did not like anybody else generally–particularly did not cotton to the Kayppock Street "dandies", who lived in the Bronx neighborhood of Woodlawn, and kept their distance.

Nonetheless, Walter Stephens was to some degree accepted as one of "us", albeit more of a second cousin once removed to the Irish neighborhoods.

"Compressed Air and Free Air Shafts, Tunnels, Foundations, Caissons, Subway, Sewer Cofferdam Construction Workers of New York, New Jersey States and Vicinity A.F.L.-C.I.O. Laborers Local 147 office, to who can I direct your call?"

"To Business Manager Fitzsimmons MacDonald, please."

"Yeah," Fitzsimmons MacDonald answered on the third ring in his gravel gargling voice, "Whadda youse want?"

"And top of the mornin' to you, Fitz. This is Walt. I need to have an important parlay with you before noon. Can you spare me a few minutes?"

"Mebbe, what's it about?"

"Not to be melodramatic, but it is top-secret, national security stuff—not for the phone. Never can tell who's eavesdropping."

"Like the mayor's office, youse mean? Youse puttin' me on, Mister Mayor?"

"No, I swear. It is a big secret, and I am not exaggerating in the least."

There was a pregnant pause.

"Better not be, and this better not be political or askin' for donations for the NYPD ball or some such nonsense."

"I'll be there in half an hour."

The mayor was driven from City Hall Park in Manhattan to Katonah Avenue and parked behind the 147 Union Building at 4332 in record time. The lights and sirens and the right to flout the traffic laws altogether was one of the perks of office, Walt Stephenson enjoyed most about his job. The building was an unimposing single-story structure built in 1985–a rectangular box shaped concrete construction with a prominent circular sign over the front entrance. Its humble appearance belied the importance of the work done inside.

On this trip to the Local 147 building, the mayor chose an unmarked police car to avoid his visit being noted and recorded by locals. He and his small retinue entered the rear door and walked forward to MacDonald's office. He entered the cluttered official's office unannounced and began speaking as if he had merely paused in an ongoing conversation as was his annoying habit.

"Now, hear me out, Fitz," Mayor Stephens said conversationally as if the union leader had interrupted his flow, "this is the thing. The Washington higher-ups–and I do mean higher of the higher ups—have an absolute deadline to complete a man-size tunnel a mile long in less than three months in complete secrecy in Mexico, just inland from Tijuana. Can you and your guys get it done?"

"Depends."

"On what?"

"Logistics and money."

"Give me the logistics first, Fitz."

"Okay. Have to get no fewer than 350 men and machines into the construction site. That will require heavy security, a good dump site for the muck, and ready replenishment of machine parts. The tunnel will have to be fairly deep to avoid creating a sinkhole; so, more time, money, machinery, and men."

"Presume for the moment that money and transportation are not an issue. Can you do it?"

"Yep. The sandhogs can do it, but it will cost."

"Okay, how much?"

"In addition to the transportation—which is your responsibility—about a million US dollars a mile, maybe more. Maybe a lot more, dependin'. And there's a ton of logistics: insurance, contracts, rounding up the help, shutting down some big operations in the city, keeping the Mexican federales' palms greased, to name a few.

Sandhogs gotta be willing to work hard, be alert and like getting' dirty; 80% of my sandhogs are eligible for workers' compensation upon retirement–mostly because of respiratory problems, and that's gotta be factored in for the long-term consequences. These guys are among the highest paid construction workers in the nation, earning about $100,000 in salary and benefits each, and they have gotta be guaranteed at least that plus special hazard pay.

"Sandhogs die in a variety of grim ways," Fitz continued. "Onna my guys was killed by a 16-ton winch that fell several hundred feet from the top of a shaft and squashed him. Another fell off the top of the 450-ton boring machine, fracturing his skull in a buncha places despite him wearing the regulation headgear. Other good sandhogs have been buried in cave-ins, crushed by fallin' rocks, and fallin' down shafts. One sandhog died after drilling into undetonated dynamite.

"The biggest threat to sandhogs, however, is not some horrific mishap but long-term, it's silicosis, a lung disease."

"I know a guy, and he can take care of all of that. None of that money is terribly important. But timing is crucial. The man we came to rescue is of supreme importance to the country. That must take place on or before September 16."

"You don't want much, do ya?"

"I do want much, and I have every faith in the sandhogs that they can get it done. Am I right?"

"Yeah. We can do it. And we will do it, starting this very day if certain conditions are agreed upon."

"Gimme the list quick, Fitz. This is urgent."

"Time and a half and another half for hazardous condition pay, nonnegotiable. An upfront inducement payment of 5K per man, including engineers, administrators, and union bosses, to see that everything runs copacetic. You know how it is for us: we lose a man a mile. That's just a sad fact; so, there has to be escrow to provide a handsome payout to the widow and orphans."

"No problem. Let's get down to it. How much for baksheesh?"

"Nothing, my friend. You hurt my feelings. Of course, you can never be sure about cost overruns, and we don't want to haggle at the end, capisce?"

"Better, I *tha e a 'tuigsinn*," Mayor Stephens said.

"Ah, good on ya. Oneupmanship in Gaelic no less. So, you understand, and we can agree."

They shook on it.

CHAPTER
SIX

President Willets, DCIA Norcroft, and McGee, met with the representatives of the Sandhogs Union to hash out logistics for the great "Ivory White" tunnel project. They were in the Russel Senate Office Building in the offices of Senator Larsen of Utah, who was on the stump at home in anticipation of the midterm elections. Larsen was a worry-wart—a Republican in the most Republican state in the union—and the only way a Democrat could be elected instead of him was if Larsen was to commit some grotesque sin/crime on the Capitol steps in full view of national television. He did not drink, smoke, gamble, swear, cavort with women not his wife, or have an offshore bank account; and he could never even feebly support a Democrat program like pro-choice, pro-same sex marriage or adoption, legalize marijuana, or come out publicly as being gay. He was a shoo-in. However, the president took advantage of Larsen's worries and encouraged him to get out and get the vote while he used the man's office suite to hold his meeting with no one the wiser.

"Sybil and McGee, thanks for coming on such short notice," the president said, "I think we are all pretty much in the know and in agreement with the plan to get Ivory out of that prison and what it will take to do that. We do have a change—an addition to the original idea—of plans that will make the whole thing a considerably larger project and with a much harder time crunch."

Both listeners were of the same unspoken opinion, "We are already pushing the expected time of completion to as close as it can come without going over and failing."

The president laughed, "I can read your minds, you know. There is a solution. We make a second tunnel with a new entrance, one that will be all but invisible. Have you heard of the sandhogs of New York?"

Sybil and McGee nodded. The sandhogs were famous historically, in the awe with which New Yorkers looked on their work and accomplishments ongoing year after year, and in print, in live theater, in TV and movies, and even in song.

"The mayor of New York and I have made a deal with the DOD, the Department of State, and the sandhogs, to get them to Mexico and get a second, secret, tunnel built on time and over budget... way over budget."

"Is it worth it, Mr. President? I mean it will be a great deal of outlay for a project to save one man, Sir."

"That one man is Ivory White, Sybil; it's worth it," McGee answered for the president.

"McGee's right, Sybil. It is also about justice, real justice, and about bringing down a totally corrupt regime at our back fence which costs us a fortune every year at the border and from the crime that attends the presence of so many illegals. It would be worth all of it to me if the only result was to show that petit dictator up for what he is and to get a new regime of democratically elected officials in place."

The president showed Sybil and McGee the hastily created masterplan for the new tunnel to be built in world-record time by a veritable army of sandhog construction men and a secret security force that was the best of the best. President Willets was determined that this adventure would not transcend into a mini-war, nor a humiliating fiasco. It was definitely the greatest risk of his political life.

In the depths of a starless, moonless night occasioned by an electrical storm over San Diego and Tijuana and helped by a one-hour blackout of Tijuana's electrical grid—for inexplicable reasons—two unmarked Lockheed C-130J Super Hercules cargo planes landed on a hastily prepared airfield built by Seabees from the Port Hueneme, California MCB base. The only landing lights were afforded by a thousand large backpacking lanterns provided by the MountainLandOutdoors Supply House located in San Clemente. No money or paper exchanged hands; but promises for military procurement contracts in the very near future were made by the three most senior defense officers in the country, which was good enough for the CEO and CFO of MountainLand.

The sandhogs–operating under one of the most accomplished and experienced tunnel diggers in the world–named Duffy MacGuire–and his longtime right-hand man, Quinn Kelly Sullivan, assisted by MCB 2 from Port Hueneme, California, led by Master Chief [E-10] Constructionman [CUCM] Ed Walker. Seabees believe that anything they are tasked with, they "Can Do"—and along with the sandhogs had the machinery unloaded from the huge planes in less than two hours. The entrance site for the tunnel was located east of Tijuana in the desert between "TJ" and Tecate, a little less than a mile from the infamous Altiplano maximum security prison. The first shovelful of desert sand was removed before the emergence of pre-dawn light.

In total darkness and near silence underground, shrouded in silvery dust, two men guided a jumbo drill boring into ancient Mojave Desert sandstone and bedrock. Sandhogs were entirely at home laboring in mud or sand and down, down, into hard rock. They drilled and dynamited as other men built reinforced concrete linings around the hole they were creating that was big enough for a large car or medium truck to pass. They employed a small TBM [Tunnel Boring Machine] 6 feet in diameter that can mine from 2,000 to 20,000 ft in open or closed mode through geology from soft ground to hard rock.

This was a small quick TBM operation which went swiftly along with hydraulic motors driving the cutterhead and manual hydraulic valve banks for machine control. Muck removal was accomplished by small tunnel fitting rail-bound rolling stock with battery powered locomotives.

The advantage of diesel power was that the battery-operated drills had reduced ventilation requirements in the smaller space, and overall costs for ventilation ducting and locomotive maintenance were reduced, a factor that pleased the cost-conscious president.

The Boretec company started to develop small-bore, hard-rock TBMs in the 2.2- to 2.4-m diameter range, mostly Double Shield models. The key to this development was to put the largest diameter cutter ring on the smallest effective bore diameter, and back it up with enough power (2 x 350 hp = 700 hp hydraulic or about 500 hp net), to get enough torque through to the cutters. These larger diameter cutters performed much better than smaller cutters that had previously been used, which were as small as 12 in. in diameter on those earlier models. The larger cutters were placed on the cutterhead with a narrow enough kerf spacing to allow for effective chipping of very hard rock.

Boretec had customized muck boxes to maximize muck removal capacity for this top-secret project. The custom requirements required enough room for a conveyor in addition to the tunnel itself. There are three main types of TBMs: Earth Pressure Balance Machines [EPB], Slurry Shield (SS) and open-face type. All types of closed machines operate like Single Shield TBMs, using thrust cylinders to advance forward by pushing off against concrete segments. Earth Pressure Balance Machines are used in soft ground with less than 7 bars of pressure.

For the sake of keeping to the rigid schedule, the cutter head employed did not use disc cutters only, but instead a combination of tungsten carbide cutting bits, carbide disc cutters, drag picks and/or hard rock disc cutters—an expensive but highly effective and efficient system. The EPB gets its name because it uses the excavated material to balance the pressure at the tunnel face. Open face TBMs in soft ground rely on the fact that the face of the ground being excavated will stand up with no support for a short period of time. This makes them suitable for use in rock types with a strength of up to 10MPa or so, and with low water inflows.

Face sizes in excess of 10 meters can be excavated in this manner. The face is excavated using a backactor arm or cutter head to within 150mm of the edge of the shield. The shield is jacked forwards and cutters on the front of the shield cut the remaining ground to the same circular shape. Ground support is provided by use of precast concrete, and when necessary in the differing consistencies of the underground soils and rocks, occasionally SGI [Spheroidal Graphite Iron]. In that situation, a special team of sandhog-built segments that were bolted or supported until a full ring of support had been erected. A final segment–called the key–was wedge-shaped, and expanded the ring until it was tight against the circular cut of the ground left behind by cutters on the TBM shield.

Urban tunnelling has the special requirement that the ground surface be undisturbed. This means that ground subsidence must be avoided. In this secret project, the second tunnel could never be discovered, because only the American sandhogs could have done it. The normal method of doing this in soft ground is to maintain the soil pressures during and after the tunnel construction. There is some difficulty in doing this, particularly in varied strata (e.g., boring through a region where the upper portion of the tunnel face is wet sand and the lower portion is hard rock.)

The prisoner secret telegram system became aware early on that something was afoot. There were reports of underground rumblings and faint ground tremors coming from the direction of Tijuana. By mutual understanding, no prisoner–not even a trustee—leaked even a suspicion of a possible tunneling operation. During the tunnel building to free El Chapo, it was generally known that a tunnel was heading for his cell. No one told any prison officer about it.

Donald and Ivory were tuned in with almost electrical interest and effort to glean as much as possible from the prisoner information links.

"I've been here long enough to know that all kinds of BS gets spread around the yard; but, I also know that sometimes it is the straight skinny. I think this is one of those times, Ivory; so, let's keep our antennas up and tuned in," Donald observed.

"Don't wanna get my hopes up too high, Donald; but, I am not gonna be asleep at the wheel the day a real opportunity comes along. I am goin' to watch and wait with real care."

"That's the right idea, Ivory, my friend. I can't help but believe that *el Dia de Independencia* will be when we keep our eyes and ears open, and our bodies ready for what comes."

CHAPTER
SEVEN

With only a week to go before the September 16 deadline, the sandhogs had only three hundred feet to go before breaking through and into the original El Chapo tunnel, about twenty feet from the opening in the prison building floor. Barring the unforeseen, they would be able to reach completion even before evening that final day.

The unforeseen took place at noon on the dot that same day. The forward cutting blades of the TBM hit something extraordinarily hard shattering two of them from the machine mounts and breaking the remarkably strong and hard blade into knife size fragments. One of those fragments hurled backwards and struck one of the specialty sandhogs installing the SGI [Spheroidal Graphite Iron] tunnel lining tearing a hole in his heart eight inches long. He bled out before his nervous system could record the injury and register pain.

Duffy MacGuire said, "We never get through a tunnel project without losing a man a mile. It's the closest you'll ever come to working on a pirate ship in modern America. Ian O'Hoolahan is our victim this time around. We'll have to get the widows' and orphans' fund kicked into gear ASAP. Right now, the problem is to get a new set of blades attached to the TBM. Get on that, Quinn," he said quietly to his number two, Quinn Kelly Sullivan.

The loss of a man was a deep hurt to all the sandhogs on the project; but–as always–they did what they had to do—got back to the job, working the same as they had yesterday; but today, they had to move a little fast. They were set back half a day; time they could ill afford. McGee re-developed the habit of biting his fingernails, a nuisance he was sure he had abandoned decades ago.

Sybil Norcroft, the DCIA, Caitlin O'Brian, McGee's associate, and Mexican Chief Inspector Miguel de Pasos-Vásquez, and their action linguistics expert consultant, Dov Cohen, drove themselves nearly to exhaustion to get a perfect—or as nearly perfect as possible—bogus facsimile of Mexican President's planned *Dia de la Independencia* oration, which had been leaked to them by the agent in Sybil's agency who reported to them every little thing that was necessary—in real time—to mimic the president— his mannerisms, hand and facial movements, and unique speech pretentiousness.

When they learned of the unfortunate death of Ian O'Hoolahan, there was sadness mingled with fear among the ranking officers. Fear—ungrounded as it turns out—

that the sandhogs would be dismayed and consider the tunnel not worth the death of one of their own, and sadness that the corruption of the Mexican elites had pushed the US government to rash action that cost the life of an innocent man—a good man. They each said a little prayer in their own way that no more death or injury would take place.

The nearer the tunnelers got to the area below the prison compound, the harder the bedrock stone became and the slower the progress of tunneling. September 5, the engineers reckoned that the were twenty feet below the prison yard, ten feet below El Chapo's tunnel, and about thirty feet from their goal. The sandhogs were unperturbed; they had faced more daunting time crunches and completed the job before the deadline and under the projected budget, not that these bosses cared about costs. As a matter of fact, this time around, the cost factor was 22 million USD for the mile of tunnel, not including the exorbitant transportation and security costs, all of which were likely to increase once the exfil of Ivory White got underway.

Even at that, it was a bargain. Sandhog engineers in recent decades had developed mechanized and automated systems to chew through deep rock or muck and immediately line an excavation to prevent collapse—all without disturbing the busy city or security important desert perimeter of the prison above. In practical money terms, that means projects that once would have taken armies of men years to dig now can advance in a fraction of the time and at much lower cost. McGee knew that and saw to it that the President of the United States knew it as well. After all, this was Ivory White they were talking about.

Above ground in a dingy little abandoned concrete plant, Sybil Norcroft, Caitlin O'Brian, Miguel de Pasos-Vásquez, and Dov Cohen, were spending a relaxing morning watching better than amateur home movies. The entire plot centered on one speech given by one man who most Americans had never heard about. There in living HD color and nearly 3D clarity, contrast, and continuity, they watched Mexican President Juan Diego Sanchez-Porteño, give the best and most stirring speech of his entire career. Never mind that it was nothing akin to the oration he had prepared and had a built-in security system that could not be turned off short of a bunker bomb going off simultaneously on the projector and on the controlling computers.

Even for the perpetrators of the linguistic action, it was mesmerizing and deeply disturbing. The video had nothing in common with the prepared political and rabble-rousing speech Sanchez- Porteño was expecting to see and wanted the huge Mexican television audience to take in. He was going to be the most surprised of anyone watching about the content of the speech he was about to make and watch, as he supposed.

Caitlin said, "I cannot see a single flaw. I think we are ready."

Dov said without cracking even the slightest suggestion of a smile, "Except in scene 85 with about eleven minutes to go, the man's left ear is somehow attached to his head backwards."

He showed them, and they were all amazed that not one of them had recognized the absurd flaw previously. He let them digest the finding; then, with what was hardly even a flip of his wrist, Dove reoriented the misdirected ear and grinned at the perfection of the result.

CHAPTER
EIGHT

September 16. The invitation only audience—all dressed to the nines—crowded into the yard area of the infamous Altiplano Maximum Security Prison and took their assigned seats in the sturdily made, comfortable, recently constructed bleacher seats. At five in the afternoon, it was still oppressively hot; so, everyone was offered iced water bottles, and a choice of free-flowing popular Mexican beers—*Bohemia Oscura* or *Dos Equis Amber* on draft in frosted mugs; the president had spared no expense. After all, it was their money having come from one of Sanchez-Porteño's special tax accounts set aside for just such occasions.

The program started only an hour late, considerably earlier than most of the attendees had expected. This was still Mexico, after all.

The live band played a loud and rousing rendition of *el Himno Nacional Mexicano* [The Mexican National Anthem also "Mexicans, at the cry of war..."] by poet

Francisco González Bocanegra which was chartered by early President López de Santa Anna in 1852 of Alamo fame.

The acoustic system was world class, something the Americans were counting on. The national anthem stirred the excited upper-class Mexican contributors—all twenty-five hundred of them.

Estribillo: Mexicanos, al grito de guerra, *El acero aprestad y el bridón,* *Y retiemble en sus centros la tierra* *Al sonoro rugir del cañón.*	**Chorus:** Mexicans, when the war cry is heard, Have sword and bridle ready. Let the earth's foundations tremble At the loud cannon's roar.
Estrofa 1: Ciña ¡oh Patria! tus sienes de oliva *De la paz el arcángel divino,* *Que en el cielo tu eterno destino,* *Por el dedo de Dios se escribió;* *Mas si osare un extraño enemigo,* *Profanar con su planta tu suelo,* *Piensa ¡oh Patria querida! que el cielo* *Un soldado en cada hijo te dio.*	**Stanza 1:** May the divine archangel crown your brow, Oh fatherland, with an olive branch of peace, For your eternal destiny has been written In heaven by the finger of God. But should a foreign enemy Dare to profane your soil with his tread, Know, beloved fatherland, that heaven gave you A soldier in each of your sons.

Estrofa 2: Guerra, guerra sin tregua al que intente *¡De la patria manchar los blasones!* *¡Guerra, guerra! Los patrios pendones* *En las olas de sangre empapad.* *¡Guerra, guerra! En el monte, en el valle* *Los cañones horrísonos truenen* *Y los ecos sonoros resuenen* *Con las voces de ¡Unión! ¡Libertad!*	**Stanza 2:** War, war without truce against who would attempt to blemish the honor of the fatherland! War, war! The patriotic banners saturate in waves of blood. War, war! On the mount, in the vale The terrifying cannon thunder and the echoes nobly resound to the cries of union! liberty!
Estrofa 3: Antes, patria, que inermes tus hijos Bajo el yugo su cuello dobleguen, Tus campiñas con sangre se rieguen, Sobre sangre se estampe su pie. Y tus templos, palacios y torres Se derrumben con hórrido estruendo, Y sus ruinas existan diciendo: De mil héroes la patria aquí fue.	**Stanza 2:** Fatherland, before your children become unarmed Beneath the yoke their necks in sway, May your countryside be watered with blood, On blood their feet trample. And may your temples, palaces and towers crumble in horrid crash, and their ruins exist saying: The fatherland was made of one thousand heroes here.

Estrofa 4: *¡Patria! ¡Patria! tus hijos te juran Exhalar en tus aras su aliento, Si el clarín con su bélico acento, Los convoca a lidiar con valor: ¡Para ti las guirnaldas de oliva! ¡Un recuerdo para ellos de gloria! ¡Un laurel para ti de victoria! ¡Un sepulcro para ellos de honor!*	**Stanza 4:** Fatherland, oh fatherland, your sons vow To give their last breath on your altars, If the trumpet with its warlike sound Calls them to valiant battle. For you, the olive garlands, For them, a glorious memory. For you, the victory laurels, For them, an honored tomb.

The excitement of the crowd was reflected in the crescendo of the singing and the addition of the tears of earnest patriots. As soon as the National Anthem ended, the crowd burst spontaneously to give voice to one of the unofficial anthems, *La Marcha*

¡Viva España!
Cantemos todos juntos
con distinta voz
y un solo corazón.
¡Viva España!

in university educated Spanish and reading from prompt notes to ensure he was word perfect, President Juan Diego Sanchez-Porteño stood erect in his best martial pose and began his well-rehearsed oration—more a rally speech ala Donald Trump of America than a presidential patriotic speech. It went exactly as he had planned it for the first five minutes, and his audience responded with a crescendo of tumultuous clapping and cheering as encouraged by scattered professional enthusiasm generators scattered throughout the excited and alcohol disinhibited crowd.

"*Mis queridos amigos, seguidores y familiares mexicanos. Me presento ante ustedes con humildad por su sincera alegría por mí como su presidente. ¡Viva México !, ¡viva la República y el Partido Revolucionario Institucional! ¡el PRI! ¡Ore por la administración justa de su presidente y todas las personas designadas!*"

["My beloved Mexican friends, supporters, and family. I stand before you humbled by your sincere outpouring of joy for me as your president. Viva Mexico!, Long live the Republic and the Institutional Revolutionary Party! the PRI! Pray for the righteous administration of your president and all of his appointees!"]

Then the wheels fell off President Sanchez-Porteño's wagon, and it figuratively left the paved road completely to crash in the brambles of the informed world.

The man in the video was the same one who started the self-serving oration; he was dressed in the same rather gaudy military uniform even though he had never served his country in its military in his life. His voice, its tonal qualities, its familiar emphases, and its accompanying facial and hand movements, showed that the attendees were still looking at their wealthy and powerful president—perhaps for life—was speaking. But what he was saying was as foreign to his supporters ears as if he had been speaking Basque to a group of monkeys.

It was evident that the televised scene had changed, and the president was talking frankly and confidentially to his known cronies from the business world—the corrupt law enforcement and senior military officers in a smoke-filled hotel bar. Despite the changes and dimmer lighting, President Juan Diego Sanchez-Porteño was still well lighted and could be heard altogether clearly.

Attendees looked at each others kerfufflement.

"*Mis queridos amigos, seguidores y familiares mexicanos. Me presento ante ustedes con humildad por su sincera alegría por mí como su presidente. ¡Viva México !, ¡viva la República y el Partido Revolucionario Institucional! ¡el PRI! ¡Ore por la administración justa de su presidente y todas las personas designadas!*"

"*Miren, hermanos, hemos tenido un buen año. Los idiotas del electorado están completamente acobardados y ni siquiera hacen preguntas sobre los propósitos de nuestro muy útil programa de impuestos. Nuestros amigos de los cárteles son probablemente los mejores contribuyentes. Sus ganancias de la ... industria del placer, la mano de obra barata que proporcionan y el mundo financiero bien engrasado que administran nos han mantenido cómodos y en el poder durante varias décadas. Escuchen esto, mis defensores de las fuerzas del orden, déjenlos en paz. Eso es todo lo que tengo que decir al respecto. Paga tus impuestos, dona a la fiesta y olvídate de la gente pequeña. Yo me ocuparé de ellos. Si los amables recordatorios no les ayudan a cumplir, entonces tengo los encantadores balnearios del Centro Federal de Readaptación Social, Ceferso 6, Centro*"

Penitenciario y Reintegración Social Ecatepec, Chiconautla, y el Centro Penitenciario y Reintegración Social Texcoco, en el Estado de México, por ejemplo."

["My dear Mexican friends, followers, and family. I am humbled by your sincere joy for me as your President. Long live Mexico! Long live the Republic and the Institutional Revolutionary Party! The PRI! Pray for the fair administration of its president and all appointees!"

"Look, brothers, we have had a good year. The morons in the electorate are completely cowed and do not even ask questions about the purposes of our very helpful taxation program. Our friends from the cartels are probably the best of taxpayers. Their earnings from the... pleasure industry, the cheap labor force they provide, and the well-oiled financial world they run, has kept us comfortable and in power for these several decades. Hear this my law enforcement supporters, leave them alone. That is all I have to say on that matter. Pay your taxes, donate to the party, and forget about the little people. I will deal with them. If courteous reminders do not help them to comply, then I have the delightful resorts of Federal Center for Social Readaptation, Cefereso 6, Ecatepec Penitentiary and Social Reintegration Center, Chiconautla, and the Texcoco Penitentiary and Social Reintegration Center, in the State of Mexico, for example."]

There was hearty applause and raucous laughter from the convivial crowd in the bar.

"I tell you, those places are the equivalent of a five-star hotel compared to Altiplano where I am going to tell a bunch of fairy tales to a lot of morons with money on September 16."

Very few of the September 16 attendees were actually morons, far from it. For the most part, they knew full well about the several riots that occurred in the private corrections system prisons which paid regular kick-backs to the ever enriching president. They knew, for example, that at the end of one attempted riot, the prison management promised to comply with the enraged prisoners' demands. However, after order was restored that day, at night the "mad cows" arrived, as the riot police are called. Dozens of them arrived at the cells firing tear gas, beating the thoroughly defenseless inmates, and then isolated them in rooms and let them starve.

In the video, Sanchez-Porteño found all of that hilarious; and, therefore, so did his audience of fat cats and crime lords. None of that was lost on the live audience of attendees at Sanchez-Porteño's political rally. Nor was it likely that the millions of citizens of the country glued to their TV sets remained content with their ignorance, including especially the members of the other three political parties and the members of the uncorrupted law enforcement, legislative, and judicial, communities. Who—after the televised speech—were rather negative in their response (to say the least) to the flagrant corruption which so delighted the president and the cabal leaders who profited so handsomely year in and year out from the ongoing criminal conspiracy headed by their elected president.

While the American video presentation of the phony bar and gathering was playing out to its rapt audience, Sanchez-Porteño screamed into a megaphone provided to him by a prison official, "FAKE!, FAKE NEWS!!, LIES, ALL LIES!!!

However, the hisses and boos welling up from the elite audience drowned out the president's increasingly hysterical protests. He could be seen, but not heard; and what the audience saw was a madman caught up in the spider web of his own weaving.

Ivory White and Donald Gutiérrez–the trustee guard— were only dimly aware of the drama being acted out above them in the Altiplano maximum security prison yard. They did recognize that whatever was going on was—in all probability—not taking place according to the Mexican president's carefully laid plans.

Donald muttered the famous line of the Irish poet, Robert Burns, "The best laid plans of mice and men gang aft agley!"

Ivory replied relating the phrase to their own situation, "So, us little mice had better get down to our own business, or our plans will not go agley, whatever that means. And we need ta start awa pretty hasty, if we're gonna escape bein' shot up."

They renewed the vigor of their efforts to move aside the bric-à-brac of several years that had accumulated in

Villalobos's original tunnel. The two convicts worked as if their lives depended on the results of their efforts—which was true—and were heedless of their growing fatigue, banged up hands, and pouring sweat. After two hours of work, they became aware that the noise in the yard had subsided, and they desisted from even speaking out loud for fear of being discovered. Ivory extracted the last long 2 X 4 from the tunnel's entrance and dropped it onto the floor below El Chapo's old cell and breathed a sigh of relief when he saw nothing but empty tunnel floor twenty-five feet below him.

The only sound they could hear was a steady deep murmur of a distant engine of some sort.

The two men shrugged their shoulders at their inability to identify the faint sound.

Donald asked, "Are we ready, Partner?"

"As I will ever be."

"Okay, I'll drop down first and see if the fall is enough to break legs."

Duffy MacGuire–and his longtime right-hand man, Quinn Kelly Sullivan, MCB 2 Master Chief Constructionman [CUCM] Ed Walker, Miguel de Pasos-Vásquez, and Jose Sanchez-Villalobos crowded into the very tight space near the front end of the TBM where the intense noise was enough to make every man nauseated and to have a global headache.

"How close are we, MacGuire?" asked Villalobos.

"No more than two feet, maybe only one. Look here, Jose,"

The image on the screen of the Tunnel Monitoring Instruments using 3D geodetics with the total station manned by a sandhog surveyor showed an irregular vertical layering measured at twenty-one inches against a black void beyond it.

Villalobos observed, "Not even two feet. We are moments from breakthrough."

"And we'll mess up your neat and tidy El Chapo tunnel, or maybe spark a big explosion," said Duffy.

He would know about such things. The man was something of a hero and a legend in sandhog history. On a cold day in New York above, a major subway tunnel a hundred feet below the East River found Duffy working in a compressed air atmosphere. Suddenly the work site was rocked by a huge explosion. The tunnel ruptured; a massive amount of air escaped; and Duffy and two other men were sucked out through the gaping hole. Both other men died.

Duffy shot through twelve feet of muddy-river bed, then through the entire depth of the river itself and onto a geyser a full four stories high above the river surface. He landed in the river and was rescued. For some unknown miraculous reason, he lived and was still working on the auxiliary tunnel to the El Chapo escape route. Perhaps the most amazing thing about the event was that the twenty-two-year-old sandhog cleaned himself of and went back to work without even changing his clothes. No one but the other sandhogs could fathom why a man would do such a thing.

Miguel de Pasos-Vásquez, the police detective, made the understatement of the day, "I trust you are going to be very careful when you break through."

Duffy smiled wryly and answered, "Like always."

CHAPTER
NINE

I t was 0210–the wee hours of September 17–when Donald Gutiérrez and Ivory White dropped to the concrete floor twenty-five below with the bottom of El Chapo's bathtub which formed the roof above. Both men knew how to tuck and roll, and neither was hurt except for some ache in their hips and knees.

"Where to now?" Ivory asked.

"Not sure. I was just told to wait here until 0230 then to make our way down the tunnel following the old railroad tracks. I was told not run and to listen carefully to any noise of any kind along the way."

"What about light?"

"There is a light switch on the wall about ten feet along the left-hand wall as we face down the tunnel. I have actually seen and felt it. It worked the last time I was down here."

"So, let's have us a nice feel." Ivory said.

Donald betrayed his identity of having lived in Sussex, England for years before his criminal past put him in prison.

"It's as black *as Itchul*," *he said.*

"I'll bite," said Ivory, "Who or what is *itchul*?"

"I was hoping you would ask; so, I could display my superior English education. British sailors—like swabbies everywhere—had the habit of saying 'as black as hell'. Around church going landlubbers, certain words were known to offend the ears of children, the clergy, and tittering spinsters; so, 'hell' was often spelled and pronounced as aitch-el, the cockney way. Hence, over time it was reduced to 'itchul' and sort of lost its meaning. It became like saying H-E double hockey sticks."

"Thanks for sharing, Donald. Good getting a history lesson," Ivory said dryly, and they both laughed.

Donald counted his steps and felt his way along for what he reckoned was about ten feet. Then, he began moving the palms of his hands in concentric circles until he finally zeroed in on the light switch.

"Got it," he said.

"Don't flip it until I have a weapon in hand," Ivory said.

He found two pieces of inch rebar nearby and handed one to Donald. Ivory held his bar tensely at the ready.

"Here goes nothing," Donald said and flipped the switch.

It sputtered a couple of times but then came on with blinding intensity. Both would-be escapees had to stand still holding on to the wall with closed eyes before they could adjust to the brilliant illumination of the well-built tunnel.

His two bodyguards, his chief of staff, and his liaison officer with the federal police, hurriedly whisked President

Diego-Sanchez out of the Altiplano maximum security prison exercise yard and into his Suburban limo before any friendly or new media questions needed to be fielded. Back in Mexico D.F., the members of the inner circle began to draw up a damage control plan.

"We must first shut down the internet until this blows over to prevent the story from going viral," Communications Director Hector Alvarez said emphatically.

"Do it," said the president, "even if the libs squawk."

"Then, we delete all copies of the fake news broadcast itself," Nicolás Delgado Cantaras, CEO of *Grupo Televisa*, S.A.B., the largest Spanish content news media conglomerate in Latin America.

Jose Luis Porteño, CEO of *TV* Azteca, S.A.B. de C.V., the *Mexican* multimedia conglomerate owned by Grupo Salinas which was second in the hierarchy of news media industries, nodded his head to indicate concurrence.

Col. Alvaro Rodrigo-Perez, General Commissioner of the Policía Federal, PF and information commissioner who acted as the president's right hand man and liaison between the federal government and the law enforcement and military ranking officers, offered another recommendation, "Mister President, perhaps it would be good to institute unspoken and undeclared martial law. Round up the dissidents and the leaders of the opposition parties, especially the PAN [National Action Party], PRD [Democratic Revolution Party], and MORENA [National Regeneration Movement], everyone of them communist fronts."

President Diego-Sanchez had had time to collect himself and to think.

He added to the flow of the harsh conversation: "Get hold of Mrs. Rosita-Torres from the PRI. Tell Victoria that I want her to set up the camps to hold the expected flow of prisoners. She will know what to do. Shut down the stock market; close the border with the EEUU, and cut off all communications with them. Kick out their ambassador, Keenan Roosevelt, and the top hundred American diplomats in the country… and go ahead and include the French, Germans, Italians, and British. While you're at it, round up all the American spies that infest us and send them packing as well. Do not give anyone any suggestion of why they are being banished. Let 'em sweat."

Mexicans are sometimes called the "*mañana*, common penicillin type drug compounds type people" because of their simplicity, inefficiency, and procrastination. No one in the civilized world made that suggestion over the next week as they watched as Mexico swiftly closed and locked its doors and clamped down on all information entering or leaving the country. It was the quintessence of efficiency.

The clamp down by the Mexican federal government was a two-edged sword. It was true that the cut-off of information links coming and going to and from Mexico was very effective. But, it was also true that America and its allies found the vacuum easy to fill with American anti-government information and propaganda and an unfettered deluge of information that discredited Diego-Sanchez and his corrupt minions, however hard the PRI and the Diego-Sanchez government tried to impede the effort. The intelligence services, newspapers, and TV, and dissident groups operating in the United States and Europe, began an unstoppable flow of unfavorable information about the Mexican federal government.

The US targeted the federal police, the federal police, association of crime lords, Mexican cartels [aka, *la Mafia, La Maña*—the skill or the bad manners— *narcotraficantes*/narco-traffickers/narcos] and the several rival criminal organizations, that had been largely suppressed by the US government in its efforts to appear to be as friendly a neighbor as possible—a practice requiring considerable angulations of the truth in order to pass diplomatic muster.

With Sybil Norcroft pulling the strings from Langley, the ODNI providing its fair share of agent provocateurs and seed money, and Lincoln Howard and Mac Young managing the necessary "dirty tricks" and disinformation services of the seventeen eager US Intelligence Services operatives and their resources, the poorly thought out and misguided International Cause Célèbre of Ivory White, was rapidly turning into a painful cold war for the Mexicans. Sybil and McGee had a brief discussion on the subject of how far and how fast this thing was advancing.

McGee asked the DCIA, "How long before this Ivory White thing becomes a shooting war, do you think, Sybil?"

"I think Diego Sanchez will be removed by the decent Mexicans well before that happens, McGee."

"And if the noncorrupt police, military, and government, officials fail to act?"

"Depends on whether or not Ivory gets out of that horrible prison or whether President Willets becomes no longer willing to tolerate the Mexican government and its ineptitude. On that day, Mexico will cease to be a nuisance."

Ivory and Donald inched along the right wall slowly to be ready to meet any surprise adversaries. It was plenty light enough, but the two men were making every effort to avoid walking into a trap set by the prison officials or the *federales*.

"*There is no place to run nor anything to hide behind. We don't have anything to use as weapons except these rebars,*" thought Ivory to himself. "*A lot of good they were going to do against machine guns and grenades.*"

Both men had the same set of thoughts; but they were in it all the way, by this time; so, they decided just to keep on plugging along.

"*I wish we could begin right now and believe in the message from the earlier set of would-be escape artists,*" thought Donald as he recalled that El Chapo had gotten clean away, only to be captured and imprisoned in an apparently even more secure prison in the United States. *Nobody is going to care two-bits worth about me if we fail at this. I shudder to think what will become of Mrs. Gutiérrez's little boy if this whole caper goes south.*"

Then, as if the finger of God appeared, a man's hand reached through the wall a yard ahead of the two cons.

CHAPTER
TEN

Duffy MacGuire decided that they were so close to piercing their way into the El Chapo tunnel that he ordered that the TBM engine be turned off. He tapped several times on the wall in head of the blades of the TBM to see if he could detect the tell-tale drum-like sound of empty space beyond the thinning wall. None of the men in the crowded space at the front end of the TBM could be at all sure. More than a few of them were partially deaf from their years of exposure to noise trauma.

Duffy picked at the crumbling rocks with his small hand pick mattock, removing a pebble at a time, listening all the while for reliable sounds of breakthrough.

Then larger pieces of stone became dislodged and fell back into the space where Duffy was so gingerly working. Behind him, MacGee said with a harsh hiss of a whisper:

"Duffy, I can see some light through your hole. You're in."

Duffy took a backward step and squinted.

"Small, but real," he said and smiled his gap-tooth grin of accomplishment.

He poked the sharp end of the mattock between two fairly good-sized stones and used it as a pry bar. The stones fell away, and Duffy thrust his fist into the well-lit tunnel running at right angles to the space the sandhogs were occupying. It was exhilarating.

"Who is this?" asked Ivory as he cupped his large hand around Duffy's fist.

"New York sandhogs, who else would be crazy enough to be here below the middle of nowhere?"

"Is MacGee there?"

"I am," came the private detective's deep and familiar voice.

"Hallelujah!" chorused Ivory and Donald. "Let's finish the hole and get the flock outta here."

"Stand outta the way, boys, we are gonna break rocks."

In five minutes, the entryway into the side tunnel was large enough to allow the two former cons to slide through. Quinn Kelly Sullivan and MCB 2 Master Chief Constructionman Ed Walker, cleaned off the last rough edges and then, the entrance was fully open and a thing of beauty.

"Local 147 Sandhogs welcome you to freedom; step right in, Boys."

They did, with alacrity. This was no time for fond embraces and emotion filled gaps of time. MacGee produced a hand-painted canvas mock-up of a tunnel wall, and two Sea-Bees affixed it to the side tunnel opening and made sure there were no tell-tale openings for light to come through and that on the inside of El Chapo's tunnel, it looked like the rest of the older tunnel. MacGee had a look from inside the original tunnel and liked what he saw, but he threw a few handfuls of dust against the canvas rendering it a decade older and free of sheen.

Duffy told Donald, "All right, me Lad, go turn off the main lights and run back by the light o' yer flashlight."

It was a two-minute effort. MacGee closed the canvas curtain, and the crew began to back the TBM and the temporary train out of the hastily constructed new tunnel. They closed the exit located between Tecate and Tijuana behind them so well that only a man standing within a foot of the opening would have been able to recognize it as a tunnel entrance. The union leader and the Sea-Bee CUCM moved their men on the double to the C-130s and got the machinery moving into the maws of the giant planes.

In less than an hour the cargo bays were closely packed with the millions of dollars of tunneling equipment; the sailors and the sandhogs were sitting shoulder to shoulder and sharing coffee and phantasmagorical stories—all factually true even if beyond belief–and the great jet engines began to roar. Fifteen minutes later, all evidence of men having worked there was gone, and the ground was smoothed so that inside a day or two of winds, it would be difficult to recognize that the ground had ever been disturbed.

Lincoln Howard and Mac Young were meanwhile motorcycling with their crews of disruptive spies around the desert landscape showing the mesmerized rural peasants and the small-town merchants the fabulously well-made video of their president hatching cruel and highly profitable schemes to perform reverse Robin Hood crimes to rob the poor to enrich the already rich. A substantial amount of money began to change hands to grease the skids of insurrection. Previously bloodthirsty political enemies, disenchanted PRI, and opposition PAN, PRD, and MORENA, parties all now were willing to accept the ages old saw that "the enemy of my enemy is my friend."

That applied to the dozens of splinter groups dotting the rural landscape: mestizos, indigenous people [Tarascan, Otomí, Nahuatl, Mazahua, and Tarahumara] in the foothills, Europeans, land owners, village merchants, peddlers, women's groups, Roman Catholics, and even Mormons from the *colonias*. An underground army was rapidly forming which was determined to make a bloodless political change but would die for a military cause if necessary.

Mexico's large and angry population of well over 130 million was beginning to pour out of the hamlets, villages, suburbs, great cities, off the deserts and the mountains, in a growing mass movement of people, all of whom considered themselves to be Mexicans first and PRIs, PAN's, Catholics, Protestants, Ancestor worshippers, Europeans, peasants, or business tycoons, second. It was a groundswell that was no longer to be controlled by the corrupt Sanchez-Porteño's kleptomaniacal PRI or crony supported government. That day was gone forever.

Mac and Lincoln now sat in a sidewalk café in Juarez in wonderment.

Lincoln said–quoting Samuel F. B. Morse when he dispatched the first telegraphic message over an experimental line from Washington, D.C., to Baltimore– "What hath God wrought?"

And Mac put it in a more down to earth query, "And what have we done?"

President Sanchez-Porteño had no philosophical wonderings. He was a through-and-through pragmatic man. He recognized that he was under attack, and every thing he and his Margarita and their family had built up over the past four decades could be taken from them. He was a thug, a street fighter, at his core; and he was determined to fight until there was not a single so-called *patriota* left in the entire *Estados Unidos Mexicanos* [United Mexican States]. He had faced career ending challenges before and always prevailed, sometimes requiring harsh measures that he had expunged from the history books.

This was shaping up to be one of those times, he mused to himself. One thing he did know was that he had to act quickly and sternly while he could still count on some of his cronies and could weather the desertion of the others—the fair-weather and fickle ones.

Sanchez-Porteño personally wanted little more than to hide away in his large and lavish official residence located on Mexico City's main square, the *Plaza de la Constitución* [El Zócalo]. But he knew that he could hold out there only so long before *los lobos* came after him. He knew that because it was not so very long ago when he was the alpha *lobo* who had come for his predecessor, and he remembered well how that had ended.

He sighed and began to do his necessary telephoning. Within an hour he had given his draconian orders to army generals, navy admirals, all nineteen secretaries of state of the Executive Cabinet, plus the heads of the federal executive legal office and the Attorney General. He issued the same demands to the heads of the Institutional Revolutionary Party of which he was the titular head–a position no one in Mexico dared to challenge–to the presidents of the *charro* [cowboy] unions, and even to the university student unions.

There was an algorithm in place for communicating quickly to the extensive law enforcement establishment. All Sanchez-Porteño had to do was to speak to six individuals to set that algorithm into motion, and that was accomplished by a conference call that included: the Attorney General of Mexico who controlled the *Policía Federal Ministerial*, PFM [Ministerial Federal Police– the premier investigative arm of the Attorney General]; the Attorney General of Mexico City who controlled the *Procuraduría General de Justicia de la ciudad de México* which, in turn controlled the *Policía Judicial del ciudad de México*, PJCM [investigative Judicial Police of Mexico City]; the general in charge of the *Secretaría de Gobernación* [Secretariat of Government] which directed the immigration officers under the command of the Mexican Immigration Service–those officers holding the right to detain suspected undocumented aliens and–under certain conditions, such as the state of martial law declared by the sitting president at the moment—may deport them without formal deportation proceedings.

In addition, Sanchez-Porteño included in the conference call the *Secretaría de Hacienda y Crédito Público Crédito* [Secretariat of Finance and Public Credit] in control of Customs officers deployed at borders and at international airports to interdict contraband entering Mexico. It had been rumored that those officers were not above a little corruption to supplement their meager salaries.

Similarly, the president of the nation spoke to his appointee, the president of the *Banco de México* [Bank of Mexico] which operates its own security division, which is charged with enforcing banking and monetary laws, including cases of counterfeiting, fraud, and money laundering—a powerful institution in its own right that was now at the beck and call of Sanchez-Porteño. He gave his brutal suppressive orders to the head of the *Policia Estatal* [State police] forces; and finally, the head of the *Policia Municipal* [preventative and municipal police forces of the municipalities of Mexico], part of Sanchez-Porteño's far-reaching corrupt system.

Ostensibly, the P.M. was responsible for handling minor civil disturbances and traffic infractions. Of the 2,457 municipalities in Mexico, 650 have no police forces. However, some of the municipal forces are large and important. Whatever the status of the municipal police forces, they were all beholden to President Juan Diego Sanchez-Porteño, who had every intention of putting them all to good personal use.

As soon as the dictator cradled his phone receiver, the algorithm moved into efficient motion: Sanchez-Porteño's message hurried out to the two federal police forces; 31 state police forces–two more for Mexico City—and 1,807 municipal police forces by launching an "Investigation" by the Executive Secretariat of the National Public Safety System. The staggering totals of people being manipulated by the presidential puppeteer showed the system employing 366 officers per 100,000 people–500,000 total. Under the efficient algorithm, each local ranking officer, comandante–equivalent to a first captain in the military—first sergeant, second sergeant, corporal, and lowly police officer, received a communiqué by that afternoon, along with every soldier, sailor, legislator, and governor.

The wheels of the anti-democratic machine were roaring into motion.

In the midst of all that frenzied activity and joy at the prospect of putting down what Sanchez-Porteño deemed to be a ray of sunshine in a Mexican sky full of dark storm clouds for him, a thunderbolt struck.

CHAPTER

ELEVEN

At 0600 on September 17, Ivory White and Donald Gutiérrez were boarding an old 1952 Ford F-1 pickup fitted out with two bench seats bound for Ixtapa at their own request; so, they could be part of the rising insurrection. They felt like they had earned the right to be in the thick of things. Mexican President Juan Diego Sanchez-Porteño was snoring comfortably in his California King-Size bed in the National Palace beside his long-time mistress, Ana Cabrara-Lopez.

Mac Young and Lincoln Howard were awake and watching the tail-end of the all-night street parade in Juarez near the US border. Chief Inspector Miguel de Pasos-Vásquez was sweating during his pre-*desayuno* exercise régimen; and Pedro Gonzales, Comandante of Altiplano Maximum Security Prison, was trying to sleep off his hang-over from the previous night's festivities.

The comandante was rudely awakened by the night corrections officer just as he thought his headache was going to subside.

"Señor Comandante, we have a problem."

"Tell me, José Luis," Comandante Gonzales groaned, "what is so important here in the middle of the night that I am being awakened as if by a herd of stupid Chinampo cattle?"

"*Lo siento*, Señor Comandante, but it is my sad duty... my, my, very unpleasant duty... to, uh, well, uh..."

"Out with it, you moron before I have you reassigned to the laundry room!" Gonzales grumped in his harshest hangover voice.

"Ees bad thing has happen'. Two preesoners haf escap-ed."

"It could have waited until after *desayuno*, Cretino. Give me names, at least."

"One is Donald Gutiérrez."

That caught the comandante's attention, and he waked up painfully with a headache so severe that he could not yet sit up in his bed.

"And?" he demanded, waiting for the other shoe to drop, hoping against hope that it was not the *norteamericano gringo*.

The night corrections officer backed away from the comandante's bed and said in a voice just louder than a whisper... "Ivory White".

"Who you say? Speak up, Cretino. Say again!"

"IVORY WHITE, the *gabacho*, Señor Comandante," and hung his head.

Comandante Gonzales was dumbstruck that such a terrible thing should have befallen him.

"*Pendejo*, tell me that you did not say, 'Ivory White'."

"But, Señor Comandante, it is heem, the very one."

Gonzales lacked the vocabulary to express himself adequately.

He replied with icy calm, "Go to the laundry and begin your assignment there. Send your number two now. He and I will start the manhunt. And sound the alarm… NOW! Cretino!"

Gonzales managed to get up and out of bed and into his pants before waves of nausea cut him down. He collapsed on his bed, pale and sweaty.

José Luis ran from the room and sounded the escape alarm, which he should have done earlier, he knew. The prison came alive and breakfast was forgotten. As many corrections officers as could be spared mustered in the yard to learn their assignments. A general lockdown was put into place, and a hurried head-count done. Only two escapees were reported, to no one's great surprise. The night officer put calls through to the national guard, the state pólice, and the Tijuana and Tecate policía as was the policy in such happenings. Less than ten minutes later, the barren desert periphery of the prison walls was filled with dozens, then hundreds, of guards, soldiers, and local area pólice, making carefully planned out grid searches of every dirt mound, mesquite bush, and dry wash.

The frightened guards reconnoitered El Chapo's old cell and the cell formerly occupied by Ivory White and

Donald Gutiérrez. Both were empty. The El Chapo cell was filled with broken lumber; the lower half of the toilet and bathtub had been crudely hacked off, and there was a huge gaping cavern that the floor of the cell once occupied. They were looking into the wide-open mouth of a large tunnel, and there was no indication of movement in it, not even a rat.

Within minutes, the escape squad appeared and dropped a ladder into the entry. The twelve men in the select unit vanished into the tunnel with M-16s locked and loaded, radios buzzing, and lights illuminating every crook and cranny. Reports came back to the officer in charge at five-minute intervals, and all of them were monotonously the same and completely disheartening to the guards and officers whose jobs, careers, and maybe even their lives, hung in the balance.

They were in a rush to get through the entire mile long tunnel to intercept the escapees, so much so, that none of the dozen highly trained guards noticed the camouflaged canvas cover to the sandhogs' tunnel. It would not have mattered other than to raise suspicion of American involvement because that tunnel–like El Chapo's original one–was empty of people and even incriminating construction equipment.

Presidente Sanchez-Porteño's affectionate slumber with his mistress was harshly interrupted by his chief-of-staff at 0611 that morning.

"*Jefe! ¡Algo importante! muy importante esta mañana! ¡Despierta, señor! ¡Apurarse! Por favor!*"

The message about waking up and hurrying finally broke through into his groggy mind. His eyes began to focus; his ears began to separate the general noise from the chief-of-staff's insistent message; and his brain slowly–very slowly–began to function.

"*¿Qué pasa? ¿Juan Pablo? ¿Qué está pasando?*" [What is it? Juan Pablo? What is happening?]

In his most rapid-fire speech mode, Juan Pablo explained, "There has been a terrible escape from the Altiplano Maximum Prison near Tijuana. Two escapees got clean away. Almost every officer in southern Mexico is there and joining the search."

The president's first thought and utterance was "Taking away my good police and army from their duty to protect my presidency? On whose orders, Juan Pablo?"

"Commissioner of Corrections, Jefe. It is a standing order signed by yourself years ago."

President Sanchez-Porteño's second—and better thought out—question was, "Do we have the names of the escapees?"

Juan Pablo scanned his iPhone for the pertinent information.

"One is named Donald Gutiérrez, and the other is called… let me see… Ivory White."

Sanchez-Porteño screamed his dismay.

"*Dios mio*," what more can happen to me today?"

The scream unnerved Juan Pablo somewhat, and he thought it better not to reply even though there was more, and he would be expected to tell his jefe the rest.

"What is that racket outside in the *Plaza de la Constitución*, my friend?"

Chanting and singing was getting louder by the minute.

"Do you want me to close the windows, Jefe?" Juan Pablo asked hopefully.

"No, let me see and hear first; so, I can decide what to do about it."

"*Quizás no sea tan buena idea, señor presidente.*" [Maybe that is not such a good idea, Mr. President] Juan Pablo ventured to say, knowing what the reaction would be when the president learned for himself what was taking place in front of his presidential residence.

Sanchez-Porteño threw open the heavy damask curtains and got the full blast of the music, the singing, and the ranting from below.

From several places, street singers with unusually good audio equipment were singing over and over again, "He was the best pres-i-dent we ever had. I don' know where we got 'im, but until we shot 'im, he was the best pres-i-dent we ever had!"

A huge crowd was gathered around a very professional band stand surrounded by huge amplifiers and electrical hook-ups. The acoustics were Hollywood or the Grand Ole Opry in Nashville, Tennessee level of clarity and volume. A live band was playing *No Es Mi Presidente*; the large chorus was pitch perfect and as clear as if a single soloist was doing the singing:

Defiant
Ungovernable

We reject him.
And we don't fear him
We choose freedom over fear
Because our futures are interconnected
Black Lives Matter
No human being is illegal
Water is life
End sexist violence

He is not my president
He does not represent the voice of my people
If you are with me say "here"
And shout, "He is not my president."
We will organize the people like always
Our power is like a current
Shout, "He is not my president."

The second verse was largely drowned out by tumultuous cheering, but Sanchez-Porteño and Juan Pablo could easily make out snippets:

… For liberation
We are the call for tomorrow…

The crowd became quieter; so, the chorus could be heard by everyone. Then, as a powerful echo, the entire crowd joined in to repeat the chorus:

He is not my president…
Our power is like a current
Shout, "HE IS NOT MY PRESIDENT!"

The president did a quick about face and looked at Juan Pablo with shining demonic eyes, "Call out the national guard! I will meet the commander on the steps of the palace as soon as they assemble. And, Juan Pablo, offer a reward of twenty million pesos [just over a million USD] from the national treasury for the man who captures that Ivory White prisoner. I want him alive. America will pay and pay dearly for his escape, and I know they are behind this insurrection. I will open the floodgates and send in tons of cheap cocaine, marijuana, heroin, fentanyl, and Carfentanil, for the weaklings in the EEUU who make all of us rich. They can't resist, and it will be the ruination of their arrogant country, all by their own choice. Get me Edwardo Machado on the phone. He will make it happen."

CHAPTER
TWELVE

Mac and Lincoln left Ciudad Juárez, Chihuahua in the north on the Rio Grande River after watching in person and on both Mexican and US television the growing insurrection. It was as yet peaceful, but that could not last, both men reckoned as the intensity grew along with the size of the crowds, now numbering in the hundreds of thousands. The going was slow—averaging ten hours a day–for almost the entire 1,100-mile drive owing to that growing multitude in every city, town, and hamlet. It should have taken them twenty hours with two stops if they could hurry. However, it took them twice that long and that many more stops because of the crowds. They did not complain, knowing that they were succeeding beyond their greatest expectations.

It was crucial at all costs that they avoid police blockades and be found out as American spies; so, they drove an old–but entirely serviceable–chevy and kept with the massive traffic crowds pushing their way towards

Mexico D.F. That way, they expected any such stops to be quickies with little close inspection.

The crowds were singing, screaming slogans, and filling the streets, heedless of vehicular traffic. The two spies elected to head west to begin with to be able to move at all, and proceeded along Calle Ignacio Mariscal, then right onto Calle Donato Guerra. The crowd thinned enough for them to reach the residential speed limit at least by the time they made it to Calle Melchor Ocampo and Calle Miguel Hidalgo. They made a steady twenty-five miles per hour as they moved further towards the outskirts of the city on Avenida Lerdo, Calle Eje Vial Juan Gabriel, Calle Minitatlan and finally onto Mex450/Libramiento Noreste de Zacataca, and then onto the main drag, Mex450 headed south.

For the next nearly 100 miles they moved nearly at the highway speed limit of 55 mph on Mex49. It was Mac's turn to drive and Lincoln's to ride shotgun and to navigate.

"Turn here," he said at MexRamp 57D, "towards Queretaro/Santa Maria del Rio, about 14 miles."

After that, they turned onto the Mex57 exit and sailed along for more than 110 miles at good highway speeds—nearly 70 mph. They had yet to encounter a police or army road block, and things were looking good. They were able to eat the lunch their hotel had made for them and to drink a couple of bottles of water.

The next turn was onto the 95-mile long Cuidad de Mexico/San Juan del Rio stretch towards the capital city. Lincoln took his turn to negotiate the more complex road system as they began to enter the outskirts of the city via Circuito Exterior Mexquense, 85D/Carretera Mexico-Pachuca, where they ran into their first blockade. The line of cars and trucks was nearly five miles long and moved at glacial celerity, which was decidedly annoying to the already fairly uptight spy duo.

When it was their turn for their persons, their photographs, and the contents of their car to be scrutinized, they were approached by a young, rather delicate, and extremely attractive young army officer, an unsmiling and serious *subteniente* with an M-16 slung over her left shoulder and an iPad in her right.

Taking note of their Anglo looks, she spoke in English, "Gentlemen, please turn off your engine. What is the purpose of your travel today?"

"Business."

"What is your business, Sir?"

"Import/export"

"To or from where?"

"Mexico City and California, mostly Los Angeles and San Diego."

"What type of products?:

"Hand made Mexican artifacts."

"Where do you purchase them?"

"From the very skilled potters and sculptors of Oaxaca, Mexico."

"Do you mean the famous *barro negro* [lit. "black mud"].

"Yes, Ma'am, we have dealt in this wonderful black clay and pottery for years. We deal exclusively with the artisans in the area of San Bartolo De Coyotepec, the best in the world."

"Did you know that the black clay is only found in that one place in the world?"

"We certainly do. Our friends there have been working the clay for generations. They are quite incredible."

"I come from San Bartolo, and my family has a large shop there. I am glad you like it. Have a good safe trip today. I am sure that you are aware that there has been some trouble further south, a prison break of international criminals. That is why all of us are out working to protect you."

"*Mil Gracias, Teniente,*" Lincoln said which earned him a flash of a beautiful smile and a quick pass through the crowd of vehicles that was beginning to be less friendly and more unruly with the military and police blockaders.

As the girl became smaller and smaller in the rearview mirror, the two men saw her fire on a Toyota pick-up truck holding half a dozen armed men in its bed. They had attempted to force their way through the blockade. The girl succeeded and killed all six blockade runners as near as the two spies could tell.

"Looks like it's starting," Mac said, and Lincoln nodded his agreement.

The two Americans witnessed one more relatively minor incident before reaching their destination in Cuidad de Mexico—the Claudio Hotel in the area of the Doctores. Rebel forces ambushed a patrol unit of national guardsmen and slaughtered a fairly large number of young soldiers before speeding away. The killers drove by the spies' car waving Mexican flags and shouting slogans including "*Viva Mexico*", "*Viva México Libre*", "*No Es Mi Presidente*", and "*Muerte a los Tiranos y a los Corruptos*".

They took a few small detours to avoid the areas that seemed like trouble could be brewing and finally moved along without interference via Avenida Río San Joaquín Miguel Hidalgo, Avenida Marina Nacional Miguel Hidalgo Blvd., Manuel Ávila Camacho Naucalpan de Juárez, and finally— after a confusing four hours—to the Doctores neighborhood [so named because almost all streets were named after well-known physicians]. The last such road they traveled was Calle Doctor Claudio Bernard to the Claudio Hotel, a 3 star, rather nonmemorable place–just what the spy trade required.

Ivory was as skittish as a two-tailed cat in a room full of rocking chairs as he and Donald weaved their cautious way through the dense traffic of central Mexico City's regular fifth rush hour of the day. Those hours were 6-9 am morning rush; 11-2 lunch rush; 2:30 to 4 siesta break rush; 5-8 early end of workday rush; and finally, 9-2:00 am entertainment hours rush.

The streets were overcrowded with police and military vehicles, foot patrols, and army units, on the march.

Ivory asked bitingly, "How do they ever get anything done? There are more cops than civilians; think we might have something to do with that?"

"Might," said Donald who was trying to drive through the labyrinth of cars, trucks, pedestrians, and law enforcement, without having an accident.

It was his first time to be at the wheel of a vehicle in over a decade, and he was rusty and nervous.

Ivory was able to navigate well enough in the very strange city to him to get the escapees to the parking area in the rear of the Claudio Hotel without mishap or being recognized from the wanted posters adorning every light pole and building wall. The poorly lit and maintained lot was the least busy place in the entire city, it seemed. They found a parking place, locked the car, and put a driving wheel club lock in place to discourage would-be thieves. They were going to be a few minutes late, but that should not discourage or annoy the CIA agents very much. These were uncomfortable times, after all.

Donald approached the attendant at the registration desk while Ivory—who would stand out like the proverbial sore thumb in almost any grouping—made a beeline for the men's room.

"How can I help you, Sir?" the attractive middle-aged Latina asked pleasantly.

"We have reservations under the name of Young, Ma'am. Our friends have probably already arrived."

"No, *Señor*, not yet. Would you care to go to the room before the others arrive?"

"Sure."

"Face ID and passport, please."

Donald was a quick and street-smart thinker.

"On second thought, I think I would like to go to the bar for a little pick-me-up. Can you direct me?"

"Certainly, hall to the left, up two floors on the elevator, and it is on your right as you step out of the elevator. Enjoy your drink."

This freedom stuff was not going to be all that easy.

Mac and Howard ran into Ivory as he came out of the men's room, and together they checked in using Howard's black government infinity card. They found Donald, and all four rode the elevator to the fourteenth floor—there was no thirteenth.

All four collapsed on their separate beds and slept clear until 0800 the following morning. They awakened famished and showered and dressed quickly to get to the breakfast hall before it closed. Caitlin texted that all was well at the office, and she would handle all info traffic for the current business venture.

Desayuno was an la carte breakfast in a private conference room MacGee had arranged from New York earlier in the week and surprisingly good: *guajalota,* or *torta de tamal* [tamale sandwich] a specialty of the capital city; an overflowing plate of *chilaquiles* [tortilla chips bathed in either a red or green sauce as preferred by the guest and topped with chicken or egg, plus *crema,* onion, and cheese]; fried q*uesadillas fritas* [doubled tortilla filled with a large layer of cheese, chicken, squash blossom, made from corn dough, then deep fried and topped with salsa and *crema];* and *huevos motuleños* [A regional Yucatán classic–two crispy tortillas topped with black beans, layered with sunny-side up fried eggs and topped with a tomato sauce, peas, ham, and cheese, accompanied by fried plantain].

MacGee arrived by rental car at the end of the meal, and the group began to discuss the business at hand.

"We are expecting a very special guest in a few minutes. How about you guys fill me in on the happenings so far while we wait," MacGee said.

Mac put it succinctly as was his MO, "The big deal was that our good American friends– Ivory and Donald–

were released from prison, having completed all the jail time they will ever see in Mexico."

Everyone laughed.

"We watched a Mexican revolution get going in real time—something like the 33rd or 34th if you count drug wars," Mac continued. "I think there's a difference this time around. Looks like almost everyone in the country is sick and tired of the same old corruption, behind-the-scenes intimidation and violence, and the fixed poverty."

"Hope so," said MacGee, "It's about time."

"So, what're we gonna do about it?" Ivory asked with an edge in his voice, one he had earned.

"Keep 'em riled up," said Lincoln, "just like we did in North Viet Nam and Syria. With a little planning and effort we can see this thing all the way to the finish line— maybe even a new president, new police force, and new senior military officers. Wouldn't that be a nice treat?"

"Wouldn't it be?" chimed in the rest of the group.

"Oh, that reminds me; and I think he's in the hall right now. Maybe the most we can do to effect a 'nice treat' is to support our guest." MacGee said with a satisfied smile.

He walked to the conference room door, opened it, reached out his hand and drew Chief Inspector Miguel de Pasos-Vásquez into the room, along with his four intimidating body-guards. There were glad smiles, hand-shakes, and congratulations, all around. De Pasos-Vásquez clasped the hands of Donald and Ivory with genuine fondness.

"I cannot tell you how glad I am that you two were saved from that dreadful excuse for a corrections facility.

Someone told me that you are going to help in the revolution, that true?"

"Um-mmh," Donald and Ivory muttered, outright humbled to think that they were in the good graces of the man that everyone in the country knew—with the exception of the current office holder—was soon to be the president of Mexico, and perhaps a new Simón José Antonio de la Santísima Trinidad Bolívar y Ponte Palacios y Blanco, famous as the great liberator, Simón Bolívar. The man himself eschewed any such references, and his true supporters and friends almost always referred to him as simply "Chief Inspector", a title he liked because he had earned it.

CHAPTER
THIRTEEN

W e have a great deal of work ahead of us. I have a big ask of the two of you. I want you to help me recruit good, uncorrupted men and women from all walks of life here in Mexico to oust President Sanchez-Porteño and his hordes of self-serving cronies. The police and military will have to undergo a complete change of personnel in the top ranks to make any progress with the government itself and all its departments from the president's office to the men who make the sewers and water supply work. I may be naive, but I think corruption is the greatest waste in the country, and if we correct it, we can become financially sound."

"I am asking something never asked before in Mexico. I am pleading with you to join me and the bands of good decent people who want an end to the thieving, brutal, lying, Mexican institutions; and I am asking you not to take any money from the country to allow us to prove to the people that we are genuine. I am not going to take a salary or pension of any kind until I am the president, and the country is on sound and honest bases from top to bottom. Are you willing to do that for me and this great country? I only guarantee you everlasting friendship from the best of the best people."

"That's the best political speech I ever heard," said Ivory. "Count me in for the duration. MacGee will give me a leave-of-office, won't you, Boss?"

"Yes, and Caitlin and I will offer our services from New York all the while you are here. Friendship with Chief Inspector Miguel de Pasos-Vásquez and the people he gathers around him will certainly be reward enough."

"Thank you, MacGee, Ivory, and Donald. You certainly live up to your great reputations. I guess I can announce formally that Donald Gutiérrez is—in real life—DCI Gutiérrez, who has been undercover for me for the past ten years, and his service has been invaluable. Here and now, I award him the Police Medal of Merit for the United States of Mexico with the Gold Medal which expresses the gratitude of the people he serves.

"Congratulations my good and faithful friend and the bravest man I ever met. As of the first day I assume office, he is to be the general in charge of the entire Mexican corrections system and will be charged with eradicating all the rascals, thieves, and brutes. Salute!"

Everyone in the room stood at attention and saluted Donald crisply.

"I always knew you were a snitch, Donald, or whatever your real name is," Ivory said, "And I owe you a few beatings, Sir."

"Ivory, I admit that you do. But would you accept a good position in the system with plenty of graft attached instead?"

They all had a long and cathartic laugh.

The revolution was short lasting and relatively free of bloodshed. In fact, the worst loss of life and wounding occurred in less than a week of that meeting in Mexico D.F. President Sanchez-Porteño became enraged at the taunting, but otherwise peaceful demonstrators on *Plaza de la Constitución* in front of the president's residence, the National Palace.

The president started it.

His patience ran out at noon on the fourth day of the demonstrations in front of his very home. He gave unequivocal orders to his chief-of-staff and second-in-command:

"Order out the national guard."

"What orders shall I give them?"

"Bleed the *traidores*. All of them. Do it now. Everyone move double time. Tell the *Guardia Nacional* [Mexican gendarmerie with national police functions] generals that this is not a drill and not a negotiation."

The *Guardia Nacional* was on the scene by three in the afternoon. President Sanchez-Porteño ordered his butler to inform the press corps of the arrival of the soldiers to protect the "national treasure—national palace" from the "mobs" and "looters". Hordes of newspaper reporters and photographers, television channel vans, helicopters, and drones, and lookey-loos with iPhones, either arrived on their own after the butler's call or were provided transportation by palace vehicles to ensure a large and friendly crowd of spectators for the president.

Mac and Howard ate capsaicin-laced tacos and tamales at one of the hundreds of small truck restaurants "invited" to accommodate the crowds, which now numbered in the tens of thousands.

"Pretty remarkable spontaneous gathering, isn't it, Lincoln?" Mac said with a sardonic smile.

"Yup. And just in time for the president to hear another rendition of *No es mi presidente* and *He was the Best President We ever had.*"

And as if on cue, the massive crowd of anti-Sanchez-Porteños, began singing at the top of their lungs and way off key, but clearly understandable.

By mobile telephone, the president gave General Abasolo the order to fire upon the demonstrators.

"Fire at will, General."

"No, Sir, I cannot. These are just common people demonstrating and doing nothing wrong."

"You defy me, *traidore!* You are a dead man. Surrender your command!"

General Abasolo did as he was ordered and did so gladly. He wanted no part of any massacre of innocent civilians.

The president next ordered General Acosta-Chaparro, then General Alemán González and got the same response. All three generals marched stiffly away leaving their men standing around with open mouths.

All of that was caught on video tape and by radio recordings. Generals Robles, Allende, and Álvarez, also declined and abandoned their posts further inflaming the irrational anger of their president. Finally, General Juan Valentín Am answered:

"Yes, my president. I will obey the command of my great and esteemed leader. Where some others see peaceful protestors, I see communist agitators, homosexual provocateurs, bands of *putas*, gypsies, and mongrel followers. I am at your command and will have my men commence firing at once."

He gave the simple order, "Fire at will. Shoot to kill!"

Within ten seconds, more than a thousand Mexicans lay dead or barely living on the hard concrete surface of the *Plaza de la Constitución*. The plaza erupted in the sounds of hell's agonies: screams, crying, wailing babies, cursing old men, and begging women, all duly recorded for posterity, the daily news, and for the enemies of the tyrannical president to use against him. The fighters recognized the horrific mistake as an effective call-to-arms that might well destroy all chance of President Sanchez-Porteños staying on in his presidency, and they began capitalizing on the mistake immediately.

The next clarion call came as crowds began moving north away from the source of the withering gunfire and towards the Metropolitan Cathedral. Shortly, its beautiful and immaculately polished marble floors were slick and ugly from the blood of more than five hundred men, women, and children, among them several dozen nuns and priests.

The reporter on the scene for *Televisa*—Mexico's TV giant and its four networks and local affiliates gasped.

"What has that maniac in the National Palace done?"

Manuel Ortiz from Sanchez-Porteños' *Azteca*, the main competitor of *Televisa*–with two networks and several local stations–said for all Mexico and the world, "*Dios mio*, the Old Mexico is gone as of this day."

Jose Manuel Calderon, the independent thinker on duty for Imagen TV—the powerful privately owned national network—which had not been the recipient of President Sanchez-Porteños' largesse over the years–said in a fury, "The blood of martyrs is on the hands of the monster, Sanchez-Porteños. Hang him from the belfry of the church. Keep records of this atrocity for the ages to remember what we Mexicans will never tolerate again!"

In the background of the stations, reporters could be heard uttering profanities and staffers could be heard crying. It was a terrible day for Mexico, and an especially terrible day for President Sanchez-Porteños, except he did not know it yet.

More than seventy-five percent of the military forces of the United States of Mexico deserted outright or offered their allegiance to the rebel militias within twenty-four hours. The better-known corrupt law enforcement officers slipped away into the hills, to the ships, buses, planes, and any other conveyance, that could spirit them out of the country. U-Haul trucks clogged the highways when all the rental cars were taken by the men and their families fleeing as fugitives from justice. Chaos prevailed from Tijuana on the US border to Chiapas on the southernmost border with Guatemala, in Suchiate, Chiapas.

Interim president Miguel de Pasos-Vásquez ordered all soldiers, sailors, and airmen, back to their barracks. Further, he ordered all partisan fighters and militias to cease raids and firing on government officials and buildings. The great nation of Mexico became silent.

Four days after the massacre in Mexico City, the television stations united to hear from the new president, the officers of the legislature, the new senior officers of the military and law enforcement agencies. All former groups were significantly depleted of officers, the corrupt ones having departed the country like rats from a sinking ship.

Chief Minister Geraldo Leopolo de Ramirez of SCJN, the *Suprema Corte de Justicia de la Nación* [Supreme Court of Justice of the Nation]—the Mexican institution serving as the country's federal high court and the spearhead organization for the judiciary of the Mexican Federal Government—stood at the rostrum.

"We are pleased to have this large crowd of true and faithful Mexicans here today to see this peaceful change of government. Our first order of business will be to swear in the interim president of the United States of Mexico. He will serve in that position until we have a formal and legal election... I think he may run for office then... who knows?"

The crowd laughed at the chief judge's humor then cheered, clapped, whistled, and tooted their approval, of the proceedings and for Miguel de Pasos-Vásquez.

Chief Minister de Ramirez asked de Pasos-Vásquez to place his left hand on the Bible, to raise his right hand to the square, and to repeat after him:

"Protesto guardar y hacer guardar la Constitución Política de los Estados Unidos Mexicanos y las leyes que de ella emanen, y desempeñar leal y patrióticamente el cargo de Presidente de la República que el pueblo me ha conferido, mirando en todo por el bien y prosperidad de la Unión; y si así no lo hiciere que la Nación me lo demande."

Translation:

[I affirm to follow and uphold the Political Constitution of the United Mexican States and the laws that emanate from it, and to perform loyally and patriotically the office of President of the Republic which the people have conferred upon me, in all actions looking after the good and prosperity of the Union; and if I were not to do so, may the Nation demand it of me.]

The cheering drowned out any other attempt on speaking for several minutes. When it began to wane, Interim President Miguel de Pasos-Vásquez, stepped to the rostrum, raised his hands to request quiet. Such was the respect for the man, that the crowd settled down with a few uttering prayers and making the sign of the cross. Noting the signs of reverence, the new acting president also made the religious sign which caused most of the crowd to bow their heads.

"My dear friends, fellow citizens of the United States of Mexico, and compatriots from around the world. It is a great honor you have placed on me and a large responsibility you have placed on my shoulders. As you all know, this nation was founded by revolution, and that is the case today. We have seen violence and corruption here from leaders, police, and military officials—all of whom knew to do better and chose to do wrong. That ends here and now..."

He was interrupted by cheering.

"This new government—largely consisting of men and women about whom you have heard little—is a true government of, by, and for, the people. I swear that with my honor and even with my life if must needs be. We will root out the corruption and the corrupters leaf, twig, branch, stem, and roots, until we work with clean fertile ground. We will find and prosecute those with past records of stealing from you, for being unfair in their dealings with you, and for dishonoring our beloved Mexico. That I do solemnly swear.

"Our Mexico is a beautiful, cultured, and rich, country; and I will do every thing in my power to see to it that every Mexican man, woman, child, and family, gets an even chance for success within the framework of Mexican law to enjoy those bounties, so help me God!"

There were more outcries of cheers, bravos, and hurrahs, mingled with praying and the motions of making signs of the cross.

"I have no illusions that the way will be easy. It will take time–considerable time—to make things right. If you grant me that time by electing me in a fair and honest election, you will see real changes. In fact, I invite you to follow the transparency of our governmental, police, and military processes, as we produce monthly reports—this time, the whole truth, open to scrutiny and criticism. Let me assure you, I am not a weakling, a peace-at-all-costs compromising type of leader. I will fight for those of you who obey the laws, work for the good of your families with honest sweat, and who also work for the common good of Mexico.

"Let me be clear, those among us who believe they can conduct business as usual by criminal means including participation in ongoing criminal enterprises, by intimidation, by corruption, and by attempting to insinuate themselves into the fabric of the government, the police, or the military, shall be stopped. They will find in me an implacable enemy and a friend of those who work with good people to make Mexico a great and respected nation.

"Thank you, my friends. Now, let's get to work."

The applause was thunderous and resonated across Mexico from top to bottom and side-to-side via television, radio, newspapers, magazines, and word of mouth. Interim President de Pasos-Vásquez had launched a revolution daring to make profound changes and a juggernaut that could not be stopped.

US President Willets sent a very public headline congratulations, an expression of high praise and gratitude for the help in saving one of its revered citizens, and a sincere offer to be of any help, the new government might need. He, his cabinet, the Joint Chiefs of Staff, the Speaker of the House, the Majority Leader of the Senate, the heads of all seventeen intelligence services, and MAPA [The Mexican American Political Association], did the same; and all of them also sent special messages in private.

All three associates of MacGee and Associates Private Investigators thanked the president for his heroic help and pledged their honor to assist him in any way he deemed necessary. DCIA Sybil Norcroft did the same through back channels to keep the working channels open and operative.

By secret arrangement between President de Pasos-Vásquez, the disgraced former president, Juan Diego Sanchez-Porteño, DCIA Norcroft, President Willets, Juan Carlos Diego Villaneuva, Chief of the Mexican Secretariat of Security and Civilian Protection and therefore director of the CNI, The President of the Government of Spain, and the Secretary of State-Director of SED [National Intelligence Centre—CNI], officially Secretary of State-Director of the National Intelligence Centre, agreed to grant Sanchez-Porteños a writ of immunity and safe passage to exile in Spain with conditions.

First, he was confined to the small mountain valley of la *Vall de Boi* [Boi Valley]. He was given the right to live in any of its towns: Cardet, Barruera, Coll, Boi, Erill La Vall, Durro, or Taull. Second, whichever city he chose, he must remain there for the rest of his life. He was never to travel beyond the confines of Alta Ribagorca County. Third, he was not allowed to move to a new or different house within his chosen city without written permission from the governments of Spain and Mexico.

Fourth, he was to make himself available to the Spanish authorities for an in-person meeting and description of his current financial and any political status once each month at a place and time of the Spanish government's choosing. Fifth, he was never to engage in politics in perpetuity. Sixth, he was required to agree never to have any association with any criminal or criminal organization for the rest of his life and his visitors were to be monitored. Seventh, he was to submit a yearly detailed financial report of his own and his family's finances.

Eighth, he was to make partial restitution for the riches he cheated the country and the people of Mexico out of—in the amount of $30,000,000 USD—an amount considered paltry by President de Pasos-Vásquez, and confiscatory by ousted President Sanchez-Porteños and his lawyers, but one that each side could live with in the interest of peace.

Any deviation from those requirements or even suspicion of doing so would result in prompt repatriation to Mexico and commencement of a lifetime prison sentence in one of the prisons of his own making.

Sanchez-Porteños finally agreed to settle in Taull, the village at the highest elevation—4,500 feet. Like the others, it was very small, and everyone knew everyone else and their business. Also like the other villages, the houses were all very similar, with no dwelling seeming to be for nobility, the nouveau riche, or persons in anyway favored by the church, the government, or for their occupation. Villager houses all had stone walls, wooden balconies, slate roofs, and all looked like they had aged considerably since being built in the 13th century. Taull–like the other quaint villages–had Romanesque churches which were designated World Heritage sites by UNESCO. All the churches are characterized by their fine-worked stone and graceful bell towers.

Only two villages had more than one such church, and Taull was not one of them. Throughout the valley during the 11th and 12th centuries, many churches were built in *La Vall de Boi*—twenty in total.

They are the purest examples of Catalan Lombard Romanesque art which came from the North of Italy.

Taull–at 4,500 feet elevation–is the highest of the villages and the most remote. It is one of the most beautiful places in the Pyrenees and one of the most isolated. There are no airports, train stops, or major highways that pass through it. It is to the west of the Aiguestortes National Park and therefore protected from development or the presence of meddlesome outsiders and is surrounded by high and foreboding mountains–which make for a highly picturesque panorama, but also a natural fortress or prison, depending on one's point of view.

Considering his other possible options, Sanchez-Porteños, his wife Portia, and his youngest son, Roderigo, were content to accept the exile with a measure of grace. They were not altogether happy with the arrangement, but all understood the grim life that would be theirs should this compromise fall through. Then, there was Sanchez-Porteños's long-time mistress, Ana Cabrara-Lopez. She was not mentioned in the deal, and the former president and wife did not so much as bid her goodbye. It was reported that she found work doing what she did best in a section of Mexico City that was not the most savory.

Sybil Norcroft called MacGee a couple of months after the international cause célèbre of Ivory White settled into its long, drawn-out mopping up phase.

"Hey, MacGee, I wanted to let you know about a new development in my life, one I have to ask you to keep on the down-low."

"Ah, oh," sounds like more cloak and dagger stuff. What have you gotten yourself into, Sybil?"

"This is political, not spy-biz, I am sad to report. President Willets has informed me that he wants me to replace V-P Broome as vice-president, since the man has been legally declared dead, as you know."

MacGee laughed, sharing a bit of serious private information with his favorite puzzle-palace director.

"Um-hmmh," he said noncommittedly.

"But, for the first while, I have to continue as DCIA until Willets can select my replacement; so, you are likely not to be rid of me for a while anyway."

"Well, Sybil, I'm glad that at least you will have some real and honest work to do. I wish you every success… now and in the future," he said pointedly without asking the question both of them knew was lurking in the background. "Please give me a heads-up when you learn any more interesting news. By the way how did Charles and the kids take the news?"

"Well, if I do say so myself, they were proud of me; and like you, they didn't ask questions to which they had no right to answers."

"Point well taken, my friend. As we Irish say, 'I wish you fair winds and a following sea, and may God hold you in the palm of His hand."

"Thanks, my friend. I'll see you around."

"Sybil, I will always help you anyway I can."

"Thanks, MacGee."

MacGee could not have guessed how soon that day might be nor how serious.

-THE END-